Niall

••••••THE IRISHMEN BOOK TWO••••••

NEW YORK TIMES AND USA TODAY BESTSELLING AUTHOR

MELANIE MORELAND

NIALL
The Irishmen Book 2
by Melanie Moreland

Copyright © 2025 Moreland Books Inc.
Copyright # 1231927
ISBN Ebook 978-1-998471-13-3
Paperback 978-1-998471-12-6
All rights reserved

MORELAND
BOOKS INC.

Edited by Lisa Hollett of Silently Correcting Your Grammar
Proofreading by Sisters Get Lit.erary Proofreading
Cover design by Feed Your Dreams Designs
Cover Images by AdShooter
Cover content is for illustrative purposes only.

Readers with concerns about content or subjects depicted can check out the content advisory on my website:
https://melaniemoreland.com/extras/fan-suggestions/content-advisory/

DEDICATION

To all you morally gray hero lovers...

This one is for you.

Go on with your badass self.

Enjoy.

CHAPTER ONE
NIALL

It had been a long time since we'd been in this position. A surprise raid, carefully planned and executed on our part. Finn tried to avoid violence, but this was the exception. We all wanted it.

Human trafficking was unacceptable. Add in the fact that the love of his life had been taken? It was no-holds-barred. The people involved with this horrific act would all be dead by the time we finished here tonight.

Bodies hit the wooden floor, the thumps almost musical as I aimed and shot, taking out as many of the human waste as I could.

Roman issued the order, and the lights came on as we tore off our night goggles so as not to be blinded.

I followed Finn as he raced toward Una. I was his right hand. Best friend. Cousin.

Wingman.

I faced the chaos, making sure all our enemies were down. Finn got to Una, picking her up, talking the whole time.

Then he called me. "Niall. Help."

I slung my gun over my shoulder and went to his side. He indicated the woman on the floor beside Una. "They have to stay close right now."

At a loss, I bent beside the woman. She was a huddled mass of shaking limbs—obviously terrified out of her mind.

I spoke so she could hear me. "I'm Niall. A friend of Una's and Finn's. I need to pick you up so we can get you out of here. I won't hurt you. Will you let me?"

Slowly, she raised her head, and my breath caught in my throat. She was barely dressed, beaten, her eyes too big for her thin face—and the most beautiful, fragile thing I had ever seen.

Those eyes were like a fawn's separated from its mother. Round, deep brown, terrified, and desperate. Her skin was stretched over her cheekbones, and her lips were chewed and scabbed. Still, her beauty overrode it all.

"I won't hurt you," I repeated. "I promise. You'll be safe."

She nodded, and I could see the effort it cost her. I picked her up, her weight barely registering. She was small—she felt fragile and weak in my embrace, stirring something inside me. Something deep and primitive. The need to protect, to kill anyone who harmed her, to hold her until she was no longer afraid, roared in me. A strange noise came from my throat, and I was sure I had startled her. But she didn't fight me, instead nestling into my torso as if she belonged there. I frowned, looking at Finn. "She's freezing."

I turned, yelling for blankets, knowing both women needed them.

I had never cared for another person. Looked after someone aside from my mother. I took the blanket and ineptly tucked it around the woman I held, hoping to warm her. Her skin was like ice, and she shivered constantly.

Una saw her brother across the area, bloodied and dying. Finn carried her over, and the woman I was holding shifted, looking their way.

She cried as she watched Una try to care for her brother, peeking up at me. "He was part of this."

"I think he is regretful," I replied. "And knowing Una and her heart, she will forgive him."

3

"She is so wonderful," she murmured. "I don't think I would have lasted much longer without her."

I looked around at the bodies piled up, the people we'd killed. I felt no remorse. Una had been kidnapped, and we had to save her. And she wasn't the only one. Tonight, we'd rescued other women, as well as the people being forced to create drugs that were being sold on our streets. It was necessary, and we had no hesitation executing the plan—or the human scum who perpetrated the crimes.

The woman in my arms shivered again, and I tucked her closer. Roman came over, looking between us. "We need to move. We caused more noise than I had hoped, and I want us out of here before someone notices. We need to set off the explosives as soon as possible."

"Right."

"There's still room in the van. One of the other men can take her," he added with a nod toward the woman I was holding.

Her grip on my jacket tensed, and she made a noise of distress, burying her face back into my shoulder. Unconsciously, my hold on her tightened, and a primal growl built in my chest.

"*No*. She stays with me."

Roman blinked and held up his hands in supplication. "All right."

He moved toward Una and Finn. Brian had died, and Una was holding him, weeping and refusing to let go. She became a lioness, screaming at Finn that she wasn't leaving her brother. Roman bent down, saying something to her that calmed her down, and she allowed Finn to pick her up. He jerked his chin toward the door. I joined him.

"We're heading out."

"Okay. Good." I wanted out of here. The smell of death was everywhere, the scent of blood ripe in the air. Although I wasn't sorry any of them were dead, I was sorry for the women we held. Finn and I were used to death. Bloodshed and violence were part of the world we lived in.

But these two women and the others we'd freed were far more innocent. At least, they had been until now.

In the van, I held the tiny woman close, meeting Finn's eyes over her head. I was certain that his grip on Una was equally as tight. I looked down, wondering why bringing her with me was so important. Why it felt as if I should be the only one who held her and made sure she was okay.

I shook my head, not understanding what was

happening. Why did I care so much for a stranger? I didn't even know her name.

I felt the drift of fingers on my cheek, and I looked down, meeting the dark, scared eyes of the woman I was holding.

"Anna," she whispered. "My name is Anna."

I must have spoken my thoughts out loud. "I'm Niall," I said, unsure if she'd heard me earlier in her terror.

She nodded. "I know."

Then she buried her head back into my shoulder, as if that was her spot.

And I was surprisingly okay with that.

At the hotel, we headed up to our private floor. I knew the two floors below us were clear and ready to help everyone we'd freed. Medical personnel, food, blankets, medicine—all was prepared. I also knew Finn had rooms for our friends and their wives so they could rest after the mission was complete.

I paused at my door. Finn looked at me. "Let her get cleaned up, and you can arrange to take her downstairs," he murmured.

I grunted, not liking that idea, for some reason. I carried Anna to the en suite, setting her on the floor.

"I'll run a shower for you. Find you some warm clothes." Reaching inside, I turned on the water and made sure the temperature was acceptable. "It'll warm you up."

I headed to my room, searching in the drawers. I had nothing to fit someone her size. When I had stood her on her feet, she barely reached my chest. And she was so...*minute.* She would drown in my clothing.

Shaking my head, I grabbed a pair of warm sweats, a heavy sweater, and some socks. At least she would be covered and warm. I placed the clothes on the bed, glancing down the hall, surprised to find her still standing where I had left her. I hurried toward her.

"Anna?" I asked gently. "What's wrong? Is the water too hot?"

Her voice was quavery as she spoke. "I don't know."

I became concerned as I saw how hard she was trembling. "What is it?"

"I don't know," she repeated. "I'm too scared to move. As soon as you left, I became frightened."

"I'm right here," I soothed, unsure what to do. "Please get in the shower. The heat will help."

She nodded, not moving.

"I'll stay," I promised. "I'll stay with you." I shut the door, trapping the heat in and turning my back to give her privacy. "I won't look."

There was silence for a moment, and then I heard fabric rustling and the sound of the shower door opening. Her fast inhale of air made me turn. "Too hot?"

"No," she replied. "It feels like heaven."

I faced the door again, but not before I saw her. Wet, naked, vulnerable. Covered in bruises and scrapes. Cuts. I tightened my hands into fists, wishing I could go back and kill them all over again. Take my time and make them suffer the way she obviously had at their hands.

"Are you all right?" she asked hesitantly.

"Fine," I muttered through tight lips.

"You made an odd sound. Like a growl."

"I'm hungry," I lied.

"Please go eat. I'll be all right."

Except as my hand curled around the doorknob, I swore I felt her anxiety ramp up. My own chest tightened in fear as if it was absorbing hers. I let go and sighed, dropping my head to my chest.

And I stayed where I was.

I led her to my room, indicating the clothing I put out, and then I pointed to the door. "I'm having a shower. Right there. I'll leave the door open so you can hear me. You get dressed, and then we'll have something to eat, okay?"

She nodded, clutching the towel to her chest. Her skin glistened, and the bruising I'd seen in the misty glass was vivid and dark.

"I have a doctor coming to see you as well."

Her trembling started again, and I stepped close. "A friend, Anna. All you will encounter here are friends. No one will hurt you. I swear it." I took her hand, lifting it to my face. "No one will get near you. I won't let them. Do you understand?"

She swallowed and nodded.

I quickly headed to the shower, anxious to wash off the blood and the smell. I raced through it, returning to her in less than ten minutes. She was dressed, looking like a child in my too-large clothes. She was attempting to brush her hair with her fingers, and I handed her my brush.

"Probably not the kind you like. I know women prefer certain brushes," I said with a smile. "But better than your fingers."

She offered me a timid smile. It changed her face, making her even prettier. She had a dimple to the right of one eye that deepened and made her look adorable. I imagined before this happened her smile had lit up a room.

I hoped it would again one day.

And strangely enough, I hoped I was around to see it.

All I could get her to eat was toast. Sip a little tea I added too much sugar to. I wanted her to eat more, but her terror lingered. She jumped at every noise, casting her eyes around the room as if waiting to be attacked. The lights bothered her, and I turned them down when she explained she needed to get used to the light again.

"It was so dark there," she murmured, pulling the blanket around her tighter. "My eyes hurt a little."

There was a knock at the door, and her eyes went wide. I stood, laying a hand on her shoulder.

"The doctor," I soothed, then headed over and let him in.

Dr. Barnes sat across from her, smiling kindly. "Hello. You must be Anna."

She nodded.

He drew in a patient breath. "You've been through a terrible ordeal, and I've been instructed to check on your physical health. Would you allow me to look you over?"

I saw her chest start to pump rapidly, the way her fingers gripped the blanket.

"I'll be right here, *mo mhuirnín*."

I blinked at the endearment that slipped out, then mentally shrugged. I was tired and used an expression I had heard often growing up. She had no idea what it meant.

But she relaxed a little, and Dr. Barnes did a quick exam, tsking over the bruises, asking her questions. He sat back, looking distressed.

"Well?" I demanded, worried.

"Physically, I am not surprised with my findings." He addressed Anna. "You, my dear, are dehydrated, malnourished, and it is indicative of the traumas you have experienced. You are rather tender on the right side. Were you struck there often?"

"He-he liked to kick me."

Rage began to boil again. I knew who the *he* was, and I could only hope he had bled out slowly, watching as his sick obsession was carried away from him.

Dr. Barnes leaned close, asking Anna something. She shook her head wildly. "No," she said, her voice insistent.

Dr. Barnes nodded and sat back.

"I don't think your ribs are broken, but you'll be sore for a while. I want you to take some vitamins, eat well, and drink as much as you can. I also suggest some electrolytes. No alcohol or too much caffeine for a few days. Lots of rest. No stress."

"I'll make sure of it," I assured him, then wanted to kick myself. I wasn't her caregiver.

Yet the thought of someone else caring for her didn't sit well with me.

He left some painkillers, a list of vitamins and supplements, plus the name of the same therapist he'd given Finn for Una. "Watch her, Niall. If she complains of pain in her ribs past the next couple of days, we'll do an X-ray."

"Maybe we should do one anyway."

He shook his head. "If I thought they were broken, I would, but I think just very bruised and sore. She will be very, ah, vulnerable for the next while."

"Vulnerable?" I asked.

"Emotional. Maybe clingy."

"I understand."

He left, and I rested my head on the door as I closed it.

I didn't really understand at all. I had no idea how to care for someone who was vulnerable. Emotional. Clingy.

Then it hit me that no one was asking me to. Now that she was clean, dressed, and had seen a doctor, I could take her downstairs and hand her over to the team. They would help her, get her back on her feet.

My phone buzzed with a message from Finn.

> Have you taken Anna downstairs?

I looked at the screen, then over to the woman on the sofa. Defenseless, scared, and unsure. But looking at me with total and complete trust.

> No. She's staying here.

CHAPTER TWO
NIALL

Finn showed up with Una, informing me she wanted to see Anna. From Anna's response to her, it was obvious the feeling was mutual. We left them together on the sofa, their hands clasped, talking quietly.

We sat at the table, sipping whiskey. Finn's gaze kept straying to Una as if he were worried she'd suddenly disappear.

"She's safe," I assured him, touching his shoulder. "We got her."

He sighed, visibly relaxing as if he'd needed to hear the words.

"I'm never letting her out of my sight again."

"I understand." I stared at Anna for a moment, meeting Finn's questioning gaze. I shook my head. "I can't get more than five feet from her and she becomes upset," I explained, keeping my voice low. "I couldn't take her downstairs. I stood inside the fucking bathroom facing the door while she showered to keep her calm."

"Una is reacting the same."

"But Anna doesn't know *me*," I replied, confused.

"Una probably talked about you. You carried her out of hell, Niall. It makes sense she feels safe with you."

Unable to stop myself, I looked over at Anna again. She glanced up, our eyes locking, and then she lowered her head, tilting her face to Una. They were both dressed in clothing too big for them. Our clothing. As if we were surrounding them even when we were ten feet away.

"Get her some clothing from the boutique tomorrow," Finn murmured.

"Yeah, already thought of that. I gave her what I could."

"Has she eaten?"

"Tea. Toast."

Finn chuckled. "These two are alike. Although I did get some soup into Una."

"Damn it," I swore. "I never thought of soup."

He clapped me on the shoulder. "You'll figure it out."

"Doc Barnes says she's severely undernourished. Dehydrated. She needs care and rest."

Finn nodded, looking serious. "She'll get whatever she needs. Una is very fond of her. Protective."

"Yeah," I muttered. "*I fucking get that.*" Finn looked at me, a smile pulling on his mouth, but he remained silent.

"Have you heard from them?" I asked, meaning Roman, Luca, and Aldo.

"A text saying it was done. They should be here soon."

"We need to meet."

His gaze drifted to the sofa. "In my suite. I can't leave Una." He stood. "Bring Anna with you. She can stay with Una."

I looked at them, holding hands, quietly talking.

He sighed. "I think they need each other right now."

I nodded. "Okay."

We met with the men a short while later. Everyone looked exhausted. Finn arranged food—platters of sandwiches and carafes of coffee filled the table.

Una and Anna were on the sofa. Across from them were Effie, Vi, and Justine—the men's wives. Finn had invited them, and it looked as if it was a good call. The five of them were close together, their soft voices a hum in the background. I knew they were offering comfort that Finn and I had no experience with.

Finn sat back, sipping coffee. "Fill me in."

"Almost everything went according to plan," Roman stated. His gaze flickered to Luca. "Almost."

"What didn't?" Finn hissed, leaning forward.

"Juan escaped."

Every fiber of my body locked down, and I gripped the edge of the table to stop myself from yelling. I met Finn's eyes, mine furious, his worried but calm.

"I thought he was dead!"

"No, the coward was pretending. He was shot and played dead. In the aftermath, he somehow got away. We don't know how badly he was hurt, but we have men out looking for him."

"Fuck," I muttered. "Anna told me he was obsessed with her. She was there for over three weeks."

"We'll keep her safe and hope he's crawled away to die somewhere," Finn assured me.

Aldo looked grim. "I hope he dies painfully."

"And the building?" Finn asked.

We kept our voices low enough the women wouldn't overhear. The men assured us the building was demolished, the bodies burned beyond recognition, and none of us implicated.

"The rumor has already started that there was a fire in the lab, and the entire place went up with them all in it so quickly that no one could escape. All Lopez's fault for having an auction in the same place as a dangerous lab," Roman informed us.

We spoke at length about the syndicate, working together, and our mutual hatred for what Lopez had represented. The sort of drugs he made and sold were bad enough. Human trafficking was something none of us tolerated.

Some laughter made us look toward the group across from us. Finn smiled. "Your women seem to be the best medicine right now."

"They understand," Roman replied, a look of adoration in his eyes as he looked at his wife.

"I am obligated to all of you," Finn said seriously. "I owe each of you a debt I can never repay, and I will be there if you need me."

Luca grimaced. "Getting rid of him was in all our best interests. But we're happy to have helped. I think this has made the syndicate tighter with a common goal. The message will be heard, however it is delivered." He stood. "But I need my wife and some sleep. We'll talk more before we leave tomorrow."

We stood and shook hands. "Thank you."

Anna shook her head. "I can't take your bed, Niall."

I lifted the covers. "I sleep on that sofa more than this bed, Anna," I lied. I was not letting her sleep on the sofa or getting a rollaway cot. She needed the comfort of the bed. The distance from the door. It seemed to bother her, although I'd shown her the proper locks and reminded her gently that she was safe. I hadn't mentioned Juan's apparent escape. I didn't want her more upset. Still, she was anxious being close to the door leading to the hallway.

"Get in," I said firmly.

She slid in, her body relaxing into the pillow. "Can you leave the light on?" she asked, sounding ashamed to ask.

I didn't want her feeling that way. She'd been through a terrible ordeal, and she needed to know where she was when she opened her eyes.

"Of course. I'll put it to low. The pills Dr. Barnes gave you will make you drowsy so you should sleep, but I'm right out there." I indicated the living area. "I'll leave a light on by the sofa as well."

I was unsure what to do next. She solved the problem by grasping my hand. "Thank you, Niall. You saved my life. I'll never be able to say thank you enough."

"I'm glad we did." I bent a little lower. "No one deserves what happened to you, Anna. You know that, right? You did nothing wrong. They were looking for easy targets, and they found you. That we were able to get you out makes me grateful I am the person I am. That I have the skill set to defend those who cannot."

Her eyes were wide as I finished talking. "I'm grateful too."

For some reason, I bent low and brushed a kiss to her forehead. "Sleep. You're safe and I'm here."

"I'm grateful for that too," she whispered, then rolled to her side, pulling up the soft comforter.

I stared down at her, loath to leave for some reason. Wanting to stroke her pretty hair and talk to her more. Let her feel the safety of me beside her. Assure her that I wouldn't let anything hurt her again.

I had to step back, shocked at my thoughts. At the fact that my hand was already reaching over to touch her.

She didn't want to be touched. She wanted a safe space, and that was what I was giving her.

Nothing else.

I turned and walked away.

The suite was quiet for about an hour. I was unable to sleep, tense and agitated. I kept seeing the barn. The darkness. Smelling the blood. Watching the bodies fall. Feeling satisfaction as they did.

I wasn't a good man. I had no remorse for the lives we'd taken tonight. Knowing that by killing those sorry excuses for humans ensured that we saved others from the same fate as Anna, Una, and countless others brought me a grim pleasure.

The thought of what they would have done to her—to Anna—made me ill. To think that her life would have been nothing but pain and humiliation. That the sweetness of her smile would be erased and her lovely eyes dimmed of all happiness made my anger burn hot again. I had no idea what the future held for her, but it had to be a damned sight better than the hell we'd pulled her from.

I flung my arm over my eyes. I needed darkness to sleep, but I refused to turn off the lamps after promising not to leave her in the dark. I sighed, finally feeling the exhaustion catching up on me.

Then Anna screamed—the sound so filled with terror, my blood ran cold. I was on my feet instantly, running. In my bed, Anna was fighting an invisible foe. Begging, pleading not to be hurt. Crying, thrashing, her fear so real, I swore I felt it in my chest.

Unsure what to do, I leaned close, calling her name. When that didn't stop her distress, I wrapped my hands around her shoulders, picking her up from the mattress, shaking her a little to wake her. I kept repeating her name, assuring her.

"Anna, *mo mhuirnín*," I begged. "I'm here. It's Niall. You're safe. I have you."

Finally, my voice broke through her panic, and her eyes flew open, wet with tears. "Niall," she gasped, looking around wildly. "I was back there. Alone. You were just a dream. I was back there!" she wailed.

I reacted on instinct, pulling her into my arms. "No, you're here. Safe. With me."

She wept into my neck, her tears hot on my skin. "It was so real…"

"No. Feel me, baby. Feel me holding you. You're safe."

She shuddered, collapsing against me. I stroked up and down her back, whispering to her. Reciting an Irish lullaby my mum used to croon to soothe me as a child. I didn't sing, only spoke the lyrics in a soft voice, feeling her relax. But she clung to me, her fingers gripping my shirt as if afraid to let go. Unable to resist, I slid my hand into her hair, the strands heavy and silky in my fingers.

"Don't leave me," she begged.

Without a word, I lifted her, then slid onto the bed. I settled her between my legs, her head resting on my chest, and I wrapped my arms around her, holding her close. I surrounded her, her small form fitting me perfectly.

"I'm staying right here. Go to sleep," I murmured. "I have you. No one will touch you, Anna."

I felt her breathing begin to even out.

"Ever," I added.

I woke in the early morning, already exhausted. Anna's night terrors were constant, even with me holding her. She would stiffen then begin to shake, and if I didn't start comforting her fast enough, the screaming began. Or the weeping.

I wasn't sure what was worse. Both felt as if her pain seeped under my skin—I could feel it so intensely. Finally, about four a.m., she sank into a peaceful slumber. In desperation, I had texted Dr. Barnes, and he told me to give her another dose of her pain meds and a sleeping tablet. That seemed to help, and she was able to get some rest.

I fell into a light sleep with her wrapped in my arms, but I felt every one of her low grunts of pain or fractured memories as she relived them. I would soothe and whisper to her, easing her fear before it took a strong enough hold to wake her.

I looked down at her, surprised to find my hand fisted in her hair, holding her tight. I had never had a woman here before. I couldn't recall the last time I had slept beside someone. And despite the reasons for Anna being here, I was surprisingly okay with waking up with her.

I carefully eased her to the pillow, sliding out from under her. I paused, drifting my hand down her hair, then tucking the comforter tight around her. I left the door open, the light on, and I grabbed my phone, making some needed calls. A short time later, I had all I required, and I checked in on her, finding her awake and looking around the room, confused but calm.

"Hey," I greeted her.

She looked at me, her hair tumbling over her shoulder, creases on her cheek from where she'd been sleeping on my chest earlier. She still looked tired, and I imagined she thought the same about me. She was shy in her response.

"Hi," she whispered, her fingers nervously playing with the edge of the comforter. "I'm sorry."

I crossed the room, sitting on the mattress. It dipped under my weight, and she shifted, her thigh pressing into my hip. "There's no need to be sorry."

"I kept you up a lot."

I took her hand, stopping her nervous movements. "Given what you went through, hardly surprising." I squeezed her fingers. "It'll get better, Anna. You need some time to heal."

She nodded, swallowing. "You slept with me."

"You were calmer when I did."

"Thank you."

I smiled, glad she wasn't upset. "I got us breakfast sent up. And some clothes for you to wear. You can shower again if you want, and then we'll go see Una and Finn, okay?"

"Okay."

I stood, holding out my hand. She took it, letting me pull her from the bed. I couldn't resist teasing her. "You're really short."

She glanced up at me. "Maybe you're really tall."

I chuckled. "I am that. You're tiny, too. I got a medium in the clothes, but I'm thinking maybe I should have gotten a small or kid-sized."

She rolled her eyes, making me snicker again. I liked seeing her impish side. "Medium is fine. I don't like things tight. And I'm not that tiny."

"I dunno. A friend of mine's daughter likes to play with these little dolls. She calls them Polly Pockets. You remind me of those."

She blinked up at me. Frowned and shook her head. Then she did the most extraordinary thing.

She laughed.

The sound was light and effervescent. Feminine and sweet. Like champagne bubbles bursting in your nose as you sipped it.

I mentally shook my head. *Champagne bubbles*? Feck, I

was losing it. Obviously, I was even more sleep-deprived than I thought.

Still, I liked hearing her laugh.

And even more, I liked that I was the one who made her laugh. It made me feel ten feet tall.

I wanted to hear it more often.

I just had to figure out how.

CHAPTER THREE
NIALL

Finn looked at me over his coffee cup, one eyebrow raised the way he liked to do.

"Rough night?"

"Jesus," I replied, keeping my voice low. "I have no idea what I'm doing. Her terror is fucking killing me. I can't take the screams...or the tears."

"Time," he replied. "They have to heal."

"How do you stand it?" I asked, indicating Una sitting across the room with Anna. "I know how much you love her. I don't have the connection to Anna you have, and her pain is ripping me apart."

"Are you so certain about that, Niall? No connection?"

I scoffed, taking a sip of coffee. "I feel badly for her. I want to help her. She obviously means a lot to Una."

He said nothing, his skeptical expression saying it all. I ignored him.

"You saw the news this morning?" he asked, changing the subject.

"Yes. The reporting is exactly what we needed. An explosion led to the discovery of a hidden drug lab. Assumed set off by an accident in the highly flammable facility. All casualties were thought to be employees but are unidentifiable." I sat back. "Those who knew where the Russians were will assume they were caught in the inferno."

He nodded in agreement. "The racetrack is closed permanently. I think the feeling is the syndicate will purchase it and reopen so they can keep track of it. Any news on Juan?"

"No sightings. We'll keep searching."

"Good."

I discreetly glanced over. Anna looked calm, happy to be close to Una. "Any decision on Brian?"

"Yes. Una said he is to be cremated, and she'll bury him with her mum and dad. She wants a private funeral. Our crew has been informed he died a hero helping us. I am doing that for her. And I already informed the morgue. It will happen quickly before questions are asked."

"All right." It made sense. Brian was an asshole, but he did save Una's life. Finn wanted to help her erase his past deeds and be remembered as being decent.

"My focus is back on the territory and the hotel. My priority, though, is Una and helping her through this."

"Of course."

He poured himself more coffee. "Una told me Anna grew up in a family that ran summer rentals. She has experience in the industry—at least loosely. I am going to offer to put her in our apprentice program here and give her a room to live in until she's ready to face the outside world." He looked over at the two women. "She helped Una. I owe her." He smiled at me. "I like her too."

"Whatever you think is best, Finn."

"Where did she sleep last night?" he asked out of the blue.

I frowned. "In the bedroom. I thought she'd be more comfortable than the sofa."

"Ah." He leaned over the table, his eyes bright with curiosity. "Where did you sleep?"

Standing, I narrowed my eyes. "Feck off. She was screaming. I had to stay with her."

I stalked away, refusing to look back.

The stupid fecker was grinning. I knew it without looking. And I had no defense because, dammit, I liked her too.

I found excuses to stay in the suite most of the day. If I had to leave to handle something, I made sure there was a man at the door. I introduced John to Anna, making sure she understood he, too, was a friend and she was safe with him. She seemed a little less tense as the day wore on, more at ease with her surroundings.

That evening, I came back to the suite after handling a problem at the casino, greeting John.

"Everything good?"

He nodded. "Roman was here. Spoke with Finn and visited Anna."

"What for?"

He shrugged. "He was only in a few moments. I assumed checking up on her."

Mystified, I went in, frowning when I saw Anna on the sofa. She smiled at me, but the tension had returned. Had Roman said something to upset her?

I sat across from her.

"Everything all right at the casino?" she asked, offering me a smile that didn't reach her eyes.

"All sorted." I cleared my throat. "I hear you had a visitor."

"Yes. Mr. Costas—or Roman, as he told me to call him."

"What did he want?" I asked, my voice a little rougher than I expected it to be. I paused. "Did he upset you?"

She swallowed. "No."

Her reply was a lie and came out more like a question than a statement.

"What did he say?"

She sighed and ran a hand through her hair. It fell over her shoulders, and absently, she twirled a thick tress around her finger. "He told me all the other women were being sent home if they wanted or to a safe place to start fresh. The workers they had held captive were given the same option."

"Yes. We'll make sure they're all in a better place."

"He, ah, asked me my plans. Said they would send me back north or somewhere else if I wanted."

I tensed. "And what did you say?"

She didn't meet my eyes. "I didn't know what to say."

"You're staying here," I replied without thinking.

"I am?"

"You're not ready to be on your own. You're safe here. Una is here. I'm here. Finn has an idea for you he will discuss with you." I stood, towering over her. "You'll stay in the hotel."

She gazed up at me, once again the trust and hope in her eyes doing something to my chest.

"If you want," I added.

"Is-is that what you want?"

I bent and pressed a kiss to her head. "Yes."

"Okay."

"Excuse me," I muttered. "I have to do something. I'll be right back."

I passed John in the hall. "You can go."

I knocked on Finn's door, glaring when he answered it.

"Niall? Everything okay?"

"She's staying here. With me. You can tell Roman to feck off with his offers. They're not needed."

His eyebrows shot up. "Is that exactly how you'd like me to deliver the message?"

"I don't care how you deliver it. Just make it clear. Tell the Italian no help is needed on this."

Then I turned and strode away, ignoring his shout of laughter.

"I'll handle it, cousin," he called. "A bit more diplomatically. But consider your territory well and completely marked."

I flipped him off and headed back to my suite, unsure why I was so pissed off.

Except when I walked in and saw Anna again, my ire melted away.

And I knew I was truly fucked.

I got her to eat some dinner. Tender chicken, mashed potatoes with lots of butter, and a rich chocolate pudding were soft items I ordered for her, thinking they would be easy for her to eat. And high in calories, given the amount of butter and sugar it all contained.

I ate with her, encouraging her with small talk. When she seemed too tired to keep eating, I slid her chair closer and hand-fed her small bites as I talked. I told her about my mum. Growing up in Ireland.

"Were you in trouble a lot as a kid?" she asked.

I grinned. "Constantly. My mum says I gave her gray hair far too young. Finn and I were always in scrapes. Back then, there was no such thing as time-out. It was the wooden spoon and my arse. And Mum had good aim, even if I tried to escape."

That earned me a smile.

"When I was older, the scrapes turned dangerous, and she hated it. When Finn left for Canada, I was lost without him. I fell into a bad crowd. When Mum got sick and he came home a few years later, she begged him to take me back with him." I slid a forkful of potatoes and chicken into her mouth. "He was already a leader here and making a lot of money. He bought her a new place and made sure she had good care, and I came with him."

"And you're still working together."

"He's my family. More of a brother than a cousin."

"What about your dad?"

I sighed, sliding her dessert toward her. I couldn't believe the way I was talking to her. I never spoke of growing up—or my past.

"He died when I was younger. Fell off a ladder at work, hit his head, and was never right after." I frowned at some of the memories. "He was a good dad. Taught me things. Warned me to stay clear of gangs and illegal activities. But after the accident, he became angry. He yelled a lot. Drank heavily, whereas, before the accident, he only occasionally indulged. He preferred tea with Mum."

I was quiet for a moment. "He died about two years after the accident. It was the men who ran the gangs who helped me to get Mum compensation for Dad's early death. I owed them."

"So, you became one of them."

"Yes. Until Finn stepped in and made a deal with them. I left and came here." I met her understanding gaze. "I was finally able to stand on my own two feet. Grow up and feel as if I mattered. Finn gave me purpose. This life gave me purpose."

She nodded, lifting her spoon and pressing it to my mouth. I had to smile over her reversing our roles, and I let her slip the spoon between my lips, wondering if it tasted so good because her mouth had been on it.

"What about you?" I asked. "You grew up on a lake, I think?"

She pursed her lips. "My parents owned a campground. It was busy most of the year. Even in the winter, there were tasks to be done. We were always busy between school and chores. I didn't have time for much else but those two things."

"Did you like it?"

She shrugged. "It was all I knew when I was young. But I was invisible. I was never Anna. I was Joe and Elsie's daughter. The girl behind the counter at check-in. Or the one helping you get water. Bill's sister. Never Anna."

"Bill? I didn't know you had a brother. He must be worried sick," I said, reaching for my phone.

She shook her head. "He died when I was thirteen. He drowned rescuing someone in the lake."

"I'm sorry," I murmured, reaching for her hand.

"After that, I was still invisible, except now, I was the sister of the dead boy. I hated it when I was referred to that way." She pushed away her bowl, half eaten, the spoon still holding a mouthful. "I thought after my parents died and I could leave, I'd come here and find out who Anna was. Find my own life. Be seen for once." Her hands started to tremble.

"I didn't think I'd be seen the way I was. And once they took me, I realized I would be invisible the rest of my life. I never regretted a decision more."

"No." I shook my head, taking both her hands in mine. "You're not invisible. Not to me. I see you. I see the sweet, funny, smart woman you are. Think of how you helped Una. She thinks the world of you. You will get through this, Anna. You'll find your place, and you are going to shine. I know it."

Our gazes locked, and I hated the doubt I could see in hers. The fear that still lingered. I wanted it all erased. I wanted to talk to her more. Get her to laugh. To see how beautiful she was when she relaxed. I wanted her to smile.

And most of all, I wanted her to smile at me.

"I see you," I repeated. "And I like what I see. You are not invisible to me, Anna. You never could be."

Then because I was an idiot, I bent forward and kissed her.

It was just a soft press of our lips, but as I sat back, I felt as if I had just been branded.

Anna lifted her hand to her mouth, touching her lips against the soft pads.

And she smiled.

CHAPTER FOUR

ANNA

Subtle shadows played on the ceiling as I lay in Niall's bed, the mattress conforming to my body in luxury and the comforter warm.

I was safe. I knew that, yet I couldn't relax. Lifting my head, I could see the sofa where Niall slept, a silent guard between me and the door. So close, and yet, still too far away.

I didn't understand my draw to him. Why his presence made me feel so safe.

I shut my eyes, reliving the past few weeks.

The moment I'd walked past a dark alley and had been grabbed. I had fought hard, but they were stronger, and in moments, I was tied up and thrown in a trunk. A needle pierced my arm, and when I woke up, I was chained in a dark, damp place, disoriented and terrified.

I lost track of time, unsure of the hour, the day, or anything. I heard noises from somewhere down a corridor I couldn't see. Smelled chemicals that made me feel unwell. I caught murmurs of conversations of other women, but when I tried to call out to them, I was punished, so I knew not to do that.

And there was the man. Young, slim, evil-looking. Always smiling with an expression that made my blood run cold. When he was close enough, I could see the disconnect in his eyes. They were icy and lifeless. He taunted and touched. Pinched and hit. He liked to kick me. Keep me down on the ground. He whispered of the pain and humiliation I would endure.

How I would belong to him. Serve him.

I wanted to die.

And then one day, they carried in another woman. Una. She was the first person I had seen other than the man and an older version of him, whom he called "Uncle." Somehow the older one scared me even more. His gaze was pure ice. Unfeeling and ugly. He laughed at my discomfort. Stared in fascination at this new woman, and with a sinking heart, I knew she would be facing the same horrific life I was now going to live.

When she woke, she was as terrified as I had been, but she had hope. She spoke of her Finn, firm in her faith he would find her. Rescue her. Rescue *us*.

She was the one who gave me the strength to keep going. Our whispered conversations were long, and we learned about each other. Depended on each other. After a visit from the men, we comforted each other. Juan, as I came to know he was called, was as evil as I feared. His uncle equally so. And when she confessed the redheaded man I had seen the day she was brought there was her brother and that he was the reason she was there, I was shocked. Her pain was so deep at his betrayal, and I had no words of comfort to offer. All I could do was hold her hand as she wept quietly.

She spoke of Finn the most. Her hero. She also talked about Niall, his cousin. How close the two of them were. Their shared traits and their differences. I felt as if I knew them, and I prayed she was right and we would be found.

Nothing prepared me for the day they rescued us. The way the room plunged into darkness. Just as I had given up hope. The sounds and smells. The men and guns.

Or how it felt when Niall lifted me into his arms, his strength and warmth surrounding me. How gently he held me while he carried me out of that horrible place.

How he cared for me after.

How he was still caring for me.

Earlier, he had informed me I wasn't going anywhere. I was staying there in the hotel. With him. What it meant, I didn't know, but I knew what I wanted it to mean. I was just too afraid to ask.

He had kissed me earlier. A soft, quick press of his mouth on mine. Meant to reassure and ease. Or, at least, that was what I told myself. It had felt like something different to me.

I slowly sat up, knowing I couldn't sleep. When I shut my eyes, the memories came. Dark, twisted, scary. Sleeping, even with the pills the doctor gave me, only brought nightmares and screaming. I reached for the water glass, not surprised to find it empty. I was thirsty all the time—they'd never given us enough to drink or eat, and now I couldn't get enough liquid, no matter how much I drank.

Carefully, I got out of bed, tiptoeing to the kitchen, not wanting to disturb Niall.

I failed.

"What's the matter, Anna?" he asked, sitting up as I crossed the room.

"I'm sorry," I whispered. "I was thirsty."

He rose from the sofa, heading my way. His chest was bare, the dim lighting playing off his muscles. His arms were massive, his torso thick. He had long legs, and he crossed the floor before I could blink.

He stared down at me, a towering mass of muscles and heat. "You should be sleeping. You need your rest."

I swallowed, my throat suddenly dry. "I tried."

He frowned, lifting his hand and running his knuckles down my cheek. "You're safe, *mo mhuirnín*. I won't let anything harm you."

"I know that." I shook my head as tears gathered in my eyes. "I know that, but my head hasn't figured it out yet. As soon as I close my eyes, I'm back there. Or I feel as if he is in the room with me." I drew in a shuddering breath. "And I'm trying to be quiet so I don't disturb you, and I'm failing at that too."

"Hey," he murmured, stepping close. He wrapped his arms around me, drawing me to his chest. I melted into him. He was so big. So warm, so safe, so everything. I couldn't describe how it felt when he surrounded me. Untouchable. Protected. Sheltered from anything that would hurt me. He eased my fears. But when I was alone, all my anxieties came back.

"You're not disturbing me. I wasn't asleep."

"Why not?" I asked, my voice muffled.

I felt the press of his lips on my crown and the exhale of air before he spoke. "I was too worried about you."

I lifted my head, meeting his gaze. His eyes were as dark a brown as mine, but he had flecks of gold around his pupils. Set under heavy eyebrows and long lashes, they were incredible. He showed a lot of emotion in his gaze, but I had noticed he was also very good at hiding his feelings.

But right now, they were on display for me. Warmth, care, and patience were all I could see. And an underlying emotion I wasn't sure either of us was ready to discuss.

"Niall," I whispered.

"Anna," he replied, his hand on my back pressing me closer.

"I only feel safe when you're close."

"Then I'll stay as close as you want."

"You stop the memories."

"Good." He eased back. "I'll get you more water."

"Okay."

"Go back to bed. You're shivering again."

I wasn't sure how to tell him it was because of how he made me feel. Nodding, I turned and climbed into the big bed. He followed a moment later, handing me the water glass. I sipped it, shutting my eyes as the cold water slid down my throat.

"I don't know if I'll ever take that for granted again."

"You will," he assured me. "And that will be a good thing. It means you will be forgetting that time in your life. Moving forward."

He slid in beside me, holding the comforter up until I lay on his chest. He pulled me close, tucking the soft material around us. I sighed as my body relaxed immediately. His arm around me held me tight to his body, and his heat sank into my skin. I traced circles on his arm, and he flexed then relaxed.

"You kissed me earlier."

"I know."

"I liked it."

I felt his smile. "So did I."

"It was my first kiss."

He stiffened. "What?"

"Well, unless you count the attempted lip-lock Tommy Jones tried on me when I was thirteen."

He chuckled, the sound reverberating in his chest and shaking me a little.

"How can you not have been kissed before?" he asked. "You're the same age as Una, right?"

"I'm twenty-six. Two years younger."

"Still," he murmured. "You're beautiful. It seems impossible."

"I was always busy as a kid and a teenager," I explained, surprised how unembarrassed I was talking to him about this. "No time for dating like other kids. I was always busy at the campground."

"No crushes? Visiting handsome young campers?" he teased.

I laughed. "After the Tommy experience, I wasn't really interested. And when my brother died, I was sad for a long time, and there was even more work. After Dad died and it was only the two of us, life was busier than ever. When my mom got sick, I cared for her until she died, then I was grieving again. I lived a fairly isolated life, and there was never much opportunity to date, so..." I trailed off.

He was quiet for a moment. "That wasn't a real kiss," he announced.

I lifted my head. "It wasn't? It felt like your mouth on mine."

"I mean it wasn't how I would kiss you if you wanted me to kiss you."

Silence hung between us. "How would you kiss me?" I asked, aware my breathing had picked up. The way his chest was pumping, I knew his had as well.

He shifted, rolling slightly so we were face-to-face. "Are you sure?" he questioned.

"Yes."

He cupped my face, stroking along my cheek with his thumb. "So beautiful," he murmured. He smoothed his hand to the back of my neck, caressing the nape gently. I shivered in anticipation. Our eyes locked, and I saw a brand-new emotion in his gaze—lust. Desire.

Unlike the disgusting feral sneer Juan had when he stared that terrified me, all I felt with Niall was his unspoken need. A new sensation unfurled in my chest. A languid warmth that filled me. A need to be closer to him.

He lowered his head, pressing his mouth to mine, pulling me close. Our lips moved together, and when he flicked his tongue to my bottom one, I opened for him.

Nothing prepared me for the onslaught of sensation as Niall truly, properly kissed me. The feel of his tongue on mine. The taste of him. How he coaxed me to kiss

49

him back, groaning as I imitated what he was doing in my mouth. He licked deep, teased, and explored. He slid his hand into my hair, fisting it, directing me, kissing me deeper, making me gasp as he slid his lips from my mouth along my jaw and up to my ear.

"That is how I would kiss you, Anna. Every time."

"Niall," I pleaded, whimpering as his mouth returned to mine. We kissed until I was breathless, almost panting, as if I'd been running for miles. Then he pulled back, dropping small kisses on my cheeks, eyes, and nose. He lay back, pulling me down to his chest. He let out a long exhale of air.

"Feck," he cursed, then muttered something in Irish.

"What did you say?" I asked.

He laughed. "Nothing, *mo mhuirnín*."

"What does that mean? You've called me that before."

"Polly Pocket," he teased.

I slapped his chest, lifting my head. "It does not."

"A version of it. I told you that you were like a little doll."

I frowned but put my head back down. He pressed a kiss to my forehead. "Try to sleep now, Anna. I have you and you're safe." He chuckled. "I'm not sure who is going to keep me safe from you, though."

"I haven't done anything," I protested.

He laughed again. "You're more dangerous than an entire cartel. You just don't understand the power you have."

For some reason, his words made me smile.

And this time, when I shut my eyes, all I saw was Niall.

NIALL

I woke up, my cock hard and aching. The same way it had been when Anna fell asleep on me. It took me forever to join her in dreamland, but I was grateful she only woke up once with a nightmare. I had rocked her back to sleep and stared down at her for a long time in the dim light before falling back asleep myself.

I had been her first real kiss. This beautiful woman lying in my arms, trusting me. A possessive, overbearing part of me I didn't even know existed roared in satisfaction. I was her first kiss.

Which meant I'd be her first everything. That only made me harder.

I shut my eyes, trying to think of something else. But all I could think of, all I could feel, was her.

The way she reacted to my touch. How right she felt in my arms. The taste of her on my tongue. The feel of her against me. How she responded. Nothing else would ever compare.

In the early morning light, I studied her. Carefully, I gathered her hair from her face, watching her. She was at peace. Resting. Her bruises were still dark but beginning to yellow and would hopefully fade soon and leave her creamy skin unmarked. She had a small nose that turned up a little at the end. I shifted my fingers through her hair. It was waist-length and straight. Thick. The color was light, almost a golden hue, with glints of lighter blond and caramel mixed in. Unique and it set off her dark eyes beautifully.

And her mouth. Her beautiful, sexy mouth. Full lips that were soft and felt incredible underneath mine. I gently ran my finger over her plump bottom lip, resisting the urge to bend my head and kiss her again.

Kissing Anna, I realized, could become an addiction.

I hadn't wanted to stop kissing her last night. But my entire body had come alive, my erect cock wanting to be in on the action, and I knew that wasn't possible. She had just been through a traumatic experience, and she was only beginning to heal. She wasn't ready— emotionally or physically. And I wasn't sure if I was prepared for the responsibility of being her first.

"*Her only,*" a voice in my head growled, which I ignored.

I stared at the ceiling. I had lost my own virginity when I was fifteen—over two decades ago. She had been a toddler then. There was a twelve-year age gap between us. It felt like a lifetime, given my world.

Plus, I wasn't into relationships. After three failed ones, I wasn't willing to try again, and I had sworn off them. I was barely into one-night stands. They left me feeling empty. Yet, I had no desire for the things Finn wanted. A wife. Kids. Forever.

Of the two of us, Finn was far more emotional, although he hid it well from the world. He had attachments he valued greatly. Once he'd met Una, he'd carried a quiet torch for her for years. He'd rarely looked at other women, and when he had tried, his heart wasn't in it. One dinner with a girl ten years prior and his heart was taken. Even when they finally got together and she walked away, he never wavered. He waited, patient and understanding, until she realized her own feelings.

I was far more dispassionate. Aside from my mum and Finn, I had never felt any sort of attachment to anyone. I had a great relationship with our cousin, Sully, but I felt a disconnect with the rest of the world. I had never looked at a woman and thought of a future. Wondered what our kids would look like. Wanted to look after her. When I pushed myself to try, I failed. Every time.

But somehow, with her trusting eyes and quiet need, Anna seemed to be getting under my skin. And for the first time in my life, *I wondered*.

I wasn't sure I liked it.

Or what to do about it.

The touch of a finger on my face brought me out of my musings. Anna stared up at me, her large eyes peaceful for the first time ever.

"Hi," she whispered.

"Hi, Polly," I said to tease her.

That worked. She smiled, bringing out the dimple high on her cheek. She slapped my chest, laughing. "Stop it."

I chuckled. "If the name fits…"

"I'm not that small."

"I disagree. I could tuck you in my pocket or sling you over my shoulder, not a problem."

"I doubt that."

I tickled her under her chin. "One day when your ribs heal, I'll show you."

The smile left her face. "Hey," I encouraged her, wanting her smile back. "Soon."

She nodded. "I slept."

"You did. You only woke once."

She furrowed her brow, as if thinking. "I sort of recall waking up. You were still holding me."

"You sleep better when I do."

"What about you? Did you get some sleep?"

"Yeah, I did." I offered her a smile. "I sleep well beside you too."

"Oh." She looked pleased. "That's good, right?"

"Sure."

"Hmm," she hummed, laying her head back to my chest. Without thought, I pulled her close, nuzzling into her hair. She sighed, lifting her hand and stroking my head. It was intimate and sweet, a warm bubble wrapping around us in the silence.

I shifted, suddenly acutely awkward as I realized my cock was pressed into her hip. And my hand had drifted to the curve of her ass. She knew I was hard.

"Sorry," I muttered. "Nature."

She lifted her head, amused. "I'm from the north, Niall. Not a nunnery. I know about *nature*."

I blinked then began to laugh. She sat up. "I know about sex and all that."

"All that?" I asked, trying to hide my amusement.

"Your...penis or cock—whatever you want to call it—and everything. We had books and the internet at school. Plus, girls talk. Just because I wasn't kissed doesn't mean I'm not, ah, aware."

I sat up too, so we were nose to nose. Her cheeks were flushed and warm, her breathing fast. My heart hammered in my chest. I stared at her mouth, remembering how soft those lips were. Unable to resist, I nuzzled them, loving the low whimper she made.

"When you're healed, we'll explore your knowledge, *mo mhuirnín.* I'll show you all about my *cock*—" I emphasized the word "—and you can tell me all about your books. And how aware you are."

I slid from the bed before I did something I shouldn't. Something she wasn't ready for, even though she thought she was.

"I'm going for a shower. I'll take care of nature there." I winked. "And I'll think of you while I do."

I left her open-mouthed in my bed.

Then I stood under the ice-cold shower, trying to ignore the voice screaming at me to return to her.

The truth was, I wasn't ready either.

CHAPTER FIVE

ANNA

The next couple of days had the same pattern. I saw Una, visiting with her. I read the books Niall brought me. Ate with him. Felt anxious when he would leave the suite and tried not to show it. He knew, though, staying away as little as possible.

He was honest with me and told me about Juan.

"He's still out there?" I asked, terror beginning to build.

He held my hands and met my eyes. "Highly doubtful. He was shot. We think he crawled away but was probably caught up in the explosion. Or if he managed to get out, he died shortly after. We have people looking for him."

My gaze skittered to the door. "If he survived, could he get into the hotel?"

He cupped my face, making me look at him. "No," he said firmly. "His face was entered into our database. Also, in everyone else's who was part of the rescue. He couldn't get near this place or hundreds of others without alarms going off." He frowned. "I saw the bullets hit him, Anna. I think he crawled away to die like the animal he was."

"Okay," I whispered.

But the nightmares returned with a vengeance, even with Niall holding me. We were both exhausted, and I wasn't sure how long we could go on this way.

We attended Una's brother's funeral, me clutching Niall's hand tightly. He never left my side, and I felt his watchful gaze on me constantly. Una was pale and sad-looking, Finn right beside her looking fierce. She was gracious and warm to everyone, thanking them, ensuring they had food and drink.

"She is so strong," I observed. "She was like that when we were captives. Always insisting Finn would come for her. Certain of him."

Niall turned, pressing his lips to my head quickly. "He wouldn't rest until he had her back. I'd do the same."

I blinked and turned to him, but he was looking around the room, ever vigilant.

Did he mean he'd look for me if I were taken again?

"She forgave Brian," I murmured. "After what her brother did, she forgave him."

"She has a big heart," Niall replied. "She and Finn are much the same."

"Like you," I insisted.

He shook his head. "I don't have the heart Finn does."

"I would disagree."

He looked flummoxed. "Why?"

"The way you look after me. I hear you on the phone with your mum. Even how you watch over Finn. Your men. I think you have a huge heart."

He frowned, shaking his head in disbelief. "Responsibilities," he countered. "I take that seriously."

"Your mum is just a responsibility?"

His gaze softened. "She is the exception."

"And me?" I asked.

He met my eyes, something in them making me catch my breath.

"I don't know, *mo mhuirnín*. I just don't know."

Somehow, his confusion only made me smile. I felt it too, so once again, we were on equal ground.

After the event was over, we returned to the hotel. I relaxed once we were in the room, the door locked. I sat down, feeling tired.

Niall sat across from me. "Una is seeing a professional."

"Sorry?"

"A therapist."

I frowned. "How does that work, exactly? I mean, I know about client confidentiality, but given your, ah, career...?" I trailed off, unsure how to ask.

He smiled grimly. "The wife of someone in the syndicate. Nothing much shocks her. But she is very good at what she does. Finn says it has helped Una already. Perhaps you would like to talk to her." He studied me. "I am aware you try to hide things. You haven't told me everything that happened all those weeks, Anna. You need to say them, get them out in the open so they can't keep haunting you."

"I—I don't want to think about some of it, never mind have you hear it," I admitted.

"Then talk to someone who has no personal involvement. Who won't want to kill them all over again," he said mildly, although his voice was rough and his eyes burning. "I can arrange it."

"Okay."

"And Finn wants to have lunch tomorrow. He has something he wants to talk to you about."

"Do I have to leave?" I blurted, scared.

"No!" He was quick to reassure me. "You never have to leave, Anna. It's a chance to move forward. I promise you."

"I want to stay," I said, hating the fact that my voice shook.

He stared at me, then leaned forward, pressing his mouth to mine. The moment our lips met, I forgot everything. Nothing existed outside this instant. This piece of time with him and me. Our mouths moving together. He lowered from the chair, kneeling between my legs, pulling me close. He deepened the kiss, and I was lost. Lost to his taste, the feel of him close. The way he commanded my body without saying a word. All it took was the press of his hand on my back to urge me forward, the feel of his fingers on my neck. So I tilted my head and he went even deeper, his tongue doing things that should be illegal. Making my body cry out for more.

Until his phone rang and he drew back, his lips wet from mine, his breathing deep. He answered, his thumb pressing to my bottom lip. "Niall Black."

He listened and stood. "On my way."

He looked down at me, regretful. "I have to take care of something."

I nodded, unable to speak.

"John is outside. Another man at the elevator. You are safe. I will not allow anything to happen to you. Understand?"

Again, I nodded. He bent and kissed me again. "*Mo mhuirnín*, I will be back as fast as I can."

And he left.

Niall looked at me over his coffee the next morning. He was dressed for the office, his suit black, his shirt a crisp white, and his tie a smoky gray with a fine white line. His hair had been brushed until it gleamed. I knew he had to get back to a regular routine, but I had to admit I was dreading the day of being alone in an empty suite.

"Finn told me Una is going to be downstairs today."

"Oh?"

He set down his cup, folding his hands and nodding. "She always liked to sit by the waterfall, curl up next to the fire, and read."

I offered him a smile. "That sounds lovely. I haven't seen the main floor."

He cleared his throat and rotated his neck as if tense. "I know. Would you like to join her? Spend the morning downstairs and join Finn and me for lunch in the pub?"

"Really?"

"Are you up to that?"

"Is it safe?"

"The entrance is guarded. The area monitored. Knowing Una will be there, Finn will watch the space constantly. He'll have extra men around. So, yes. Very safe."

"I'd like to."

"Okay. Eat your breakfast, and I'll escort you down."

I looked at my plate. The fluffy pancakes and bacon had held no interest for me earlier. But I knew if I ate them, he would be pleased.

It should have frightened me how much I wanted to please him, considering what I had gone through. Except I knew Niall being pleased simply meant a warm hug and his smile.

Maybe another one of his drugging kisses.

So, I picked up my fork and ate.

NIALL

I took Anna downstairs, a pit of worry in my stomach. Everything I had told her was true. The area was monitored. There were guards. Probably more than I knew about since Una was away from Finn's side. He would take no chances.

Anna was calm, although her grip on my hand grew tighter as we walked across the lobby. She sat next to Una, the two of them hugging. I noticed Una's blanket and cursed myself for not thinking of bringing one, then Una grinned and unfolded the large fuzzy material and offered half to Anna, who took it, smiling.

I rested my hand on her shoulder, bending down. "If it's too much, call me." I indicated the cell phone I had given her earlier. "Or text. I'll come get you."

She patted my hand. "I'm fine. Really. I'll see you later, okay?"

I nodded and headed across the lobby. I stopped at the front desk to say hello, casually glancing back, then again at the concierge desk. Anna and Una were already drinking tea, and a plate of toast and sweet buns was in front of them, so I knew they were looked after. I headed to the elevator but paused around the corner, checking one last time. Anna was smiling at something Una said, a slice of toast in her hand. I swept the lobby, noting the men I could see, the fact that only one door was being used for entrance, and I shook my head. Finn had it all in hand. I knew he would, but I felt better checking, even with the news I'd had earlier.

In the office, I nodded at Finn, poured a coffee, and strolled to his desk. I paused, lifting my mug to my mouth as I looked at the monitors. The lobby was steady with guests coming and going. The casino was quiet this time of day. I stared at the image of Anna a beat too long, then sat down across from Finn. I had information to tell him that would help us both relax. I set my coffee cup on his desk.

"I have news."

He sat back. "Let me hear it."

"I got a call early this morning. Our contact at the cop shop told me they found a body about a mile from the racetrack."

"Juan?"

I nodded. "They think so. General description fits." I picked up my cup. "Died from blood loss. There was a bullet hole."

"Can they do DNA? Fingerprints?"

"They tried. No hits, but he was an unknown. He called Lopez his uncle, but that wasn't his real name. Could have been a son or a cousin or just some kid he recruited." I took a sip. "Fingerprints aren't, ah, possible."

"Why?"

"His right arm is mostly missing—and part of his left. And his leg was being chewed on."

Finn grimaced. "Part of me hopes he was still alive when they started chewing."

"I have to agree." I cleared my throat. "And our guy said he was wearing red sneakers. The same ones we saw Juan wearing with the tiger embroidery."

"Another clue pointing to the right conclusion." Finn was quiet for a moment. "He was shot. I saw him go down. It has to be him."

"Too close not to be."

"Have you told Anna?"

"Not yet. I will later. It might help her relax, knowing he's not out there."

"I'm going to talk to her later about my idea. Tell her she can stay in a room here until she's on her feet and feels safe to live elsewhere."

I rotated my shoulders. "Yeah, about that. She doesn't need the room."

Finn did the eyebrow lift. "Oh, why is that?"

"She can have Mum's room."

The bastard smirked. "You mean the adjoining room to yours?"

"She'd feel safer being beside me. It's private—she can keep the door locked. But I'd be close if she needed me."

"Will it be locked on your side?" he asked, still amused.

I narrowed my eyes in warning. "I'm doing this because she is Una's friend. To help."

"Right. Of course. *Una's friend*. To help."

I leaned forward, lowering my voice. "I haven't shot anyone for a few days now, Finn. My finger is suddenly feeling itchy. You want to risk it?"

He wasn't the least bit worried, instead pointing to the monitor.

"She's lovely, Niall. Intelligent. Sweet. Roisin would love her."

"I don't do relationships, Finn. I'm simply doing my part."

69

"So, you're not attracted to her?"

I opened my mouth to tell him off, but he waved his finger at me. "Truth."

"You can't help but be attracted to her," I huffed. "She's incredible. But not for me. I'm not interested in something serious. And she's the serious sort of girl."

He picked up his phone and scrolled through it.

"What are you doing?" I asked, annoyed.

"Marking today on my calendar."

"What the hell for?"

"I'll be reminding you of this stupid conversation, and I want you to know the date you denied how you feel."

"I can't deny something that's not there."

"You have no feelings for her?" he asked. "None?"

"Aside from concern, no," I lied. But I was unable to stop myself from checking the monitor again.

"Well then, working with her, sleeping that close, shouldn't be a problem, should it?"

I stood. "I'm out of here. I have things to do."

I had some people to see. Employees to talk to. But without thought, I punched the lobby and was halfway across it before I realized what I was doing. As

I passed one of the cameras, I flipped Finn the bird, certain he was checking.

The fecker.

I headed toward Anna, loving the fact that she smiled when she saw me coming. A warm, wide smile that welcomed me. Drew me in. I felt my own mouth return her smile, and, unable to stop myself, I threw her a wink. The way her cheeks darkened a little made me know she was pleased.

Which made me incredibly happy.

And I knew Finn was watching the whole damn thing, laughing, and adding notes to his calendar entry.

I hated it when the bastard was right.

And that I would have to disappoint him.

I looked at Anna.

And her.

CHAPTER SIX
ANNA

I enjoyed spending time with Una. She was funny and sweet. Our shared terror had made us familiar fast, and I was glad that closeness lingered.

We chatted about the hotel for a while, and she told me all about the renovations. I could see why she loved sitting here. The sound of the waterfall and the play of the fire on the rocks was peaceful. I leaned forward and poured some more tea.

"How are you doing?" I asked. "With the funeral and everything."

She sighed, rolling the soft fabric of the blanket between her fingers. "All right. Finn is helping. I'm mourning the loss of my brother, not the man he had become."

"You forgave him, though, in the end."

She nodded, a glimmer of tears in her eyes. "I did. I still love my brother, and I will miss him."

"And the, ah, other? Niall said you were talking to a therapist?"

"Yes. It helps. I slept better last night." She smiled sadly, sharing a look with me only we would understand. "I can say things to her I can't say to Finn. He would go mental."

"I understand. There are moments from that place I can't tell Niall about."

She squeezed my hand. "You should talk to Nadia. She's great. She gave me some coping mechanisms to try too."

"I think I will."

We sipped our tea, enjoying our quiet companionship.

"We need to go look in the shop. They got some new things in I think you'd like," she said, peering over my shoulder.

"Oh, ah, no. It's fine."

"You need some clothes."

I swallowed. "I, ah, don't have any way to pay for them right now. They took my purse with my wallet and credit card. My passport and all my ID were in it. I have to figure out how to get it all redone."

Una waved her hand. "Finn insists. I'll get some things too. Please. He wants to do this for you." She tilted her head. "He knows we got close and looked after each other. He's grateful, and he wants to do something for you."

I laughed. "I'm living in his hotel, eating his food, taking up Niall's time. He is doing plenty."

She shook her head. "Please. For me, then."

I sighed and relented. "A couple of things."

She clapped her hands. "Awesome."

We went shopping then headed upstairs to meet Finn and Niall for a late lunch. The pub was warm and welcoming, another large fireplace roaring in the corner, heavy wooden tables and comfy bench seats everywhere. Finn was waiting, and a few moments after we sat down, Niall strode in, his eyes instantly finding mine. I swore his shoulders relaxed as soon as he saw me.

I know mine did.

He sat on the chair next to me, leaning over and speaking quietly. "All right, *mo mhuirnín?*"

"I'm fine. I had a good morning with Una."

"Great."

Finn highly recommended the Irish stew and brown bread, so we all ordered it. The meat was fork-tender, the vegetables delicious, and the gravy rich and thick. Perfect to soak up with the warm bread. Finn shared stories of the hotel and a few from growing up in Ireland. Niall joined in, the two of them kibitzing and teasing. It made me laugh more than once, and I enjoyed myself.

"One time, Niall and I were about eight, I think," Finn said with a grin. "Our neighbor, who no one liked, had a pile of manure delivered for his garden."

Niall snickered. "Old man Murtagh."

Finn chuckled. "We snuck out that night and pelted his house with the manure, thinking it would be funny. We thought we'd do it in the dark and no one would know it was us."

"And?" Una asked.

"Next morning, Murtagh was yelling outside, and Mum burst into our room, screaming at us and calling us little feckers, chasing us with the wooden spoon, threatening to lock us up," Niall said, wiping at his eyes. "We kept saying it wasn't us. But..." He trailed off, laughing too hard to keep talking.

"We never thought about the smell. We washed our hands in the well, but it was on our shoes and bits on our clothes," Finn explained. "The room stank like shite. So did we."

"What happened?" I asked.

"Mum beat our arses, and then we had to go clean his house." Finn sighed. "But we got ours in the end."

"What did you do?"

"We snuck some of the wet manure into his back seat and hid it. He could never get the smell out."

We all laughed, and Una shook her head. "Poor Roisin."

I touched Niall's hand. "Your accent is heavier than Finn's," I said. "Most of the time."

He chuckled, flipping his hand over and squeezing my fingers. "Finn's been here longer than I have. He's lost a bit more of the brogue." He winked at me. "Most of the time?"

I nodded. "When either of you is angry or upset, it's heavier and you say feck instead of fuck. Or when you're laughing and talking about Ireland."

Una grinned. "When Finn is being passionate, it becomes quite pronounced. Very, ah, hard."

He laughed, wrapping an arm around her. "Quite," he said. "Very hard."

I had to look down, laughing into my napkin at her teasing.

She leaned close. "You'll have to let me know if you hear a difference."

I felt my eyes widen. Niall sputtered.

Finn started to laugh.

"Fecker," Niall muttered.

"Like that," I pointed out.

Then we were all laughing.

The waiter brought over coffee, and Finn cleared his throat, addressing me. He told me about the chance to work in the hotel, learn and be paid at the same time. I was surprised at the magnanimous gesture, feeling somewhat overwhelmed. He mistook my surprise as being distraught.

"It's only an offer, Anna," he explained, his voice gentle. "Maybe you had plans to return up north or another idea?"

"Oh no," I said. "I had been dreading trying to find a job, and I would love to stay here. I'd get to work with Una?"

"Yes, and the other staff. You'd be in guest services. Trained and paid while doing so." Finn looked at Niall, indicating he should join in the conversation.

"And you'd get to live in the hotel," Niall added, turning to me.

"I would?"

Finn cleared his throat. "I'm indebted to you, Anna. You and Una developed a friendship while you were, ah, trapped. She told me if it weren't for you, she would have gone mad."

"She was equally good to me," I replied. "She tried to protect me from, um, *him*."

My hand was shaking as I reached for my coffee. Simply thinking of Juan upset me. Niall shifted closer, draping his arm over the back of my chair.

"He can't hurt you anymore," he assured me.

"But what if he comes looking for me?" I asked, worried. "And hurts Una? I can't stay here and risk that."

Niall and Finn exchanged a look, and Finn nodded. Leaning forward, Niall spoke quietly, telling Una and me that Juan was dead.

"You're sure?" I asked, my voice thick.

"They can't ID him since there was no way to fingerprint him and no DNA in any system. But the fact that he was so close to the track and had a gunshot, the coincidence is too great," Finn replied with confidence. "Plus, he was wearing those hideous sneakers."

"Why no fingerprints?" Una asked.

Finn cleared his throat. "Mother Nature has a way of removing them."

Una looked puzzled, then her eyes went wide. "Oh. *Oh.*"

Confused, I looked at her, and Una mimed biting her nails. Theatrically. For a moment, I was startled, and then I turned my face, coughing to cover a little laugh. One animal destroyed by another one.

"He deserved it," Una stated.

I nodded, shifting in my chair to face Niall. I felt his hands playing in my hair, trying to comfort me.

"Maybe we should discuss it?" I asked.

"It's your decision. I think you'd like it here. Great staff. And you'd be safe." His gaze was reassuring, and I had the feeling he wanted me to take the offer.

I turned back to Finn. "I accept."

"Great. I'll get the paperwork in order with HR. You can take a little more time to recover and start next week."

"Okay."

Niall stood. "You look pale and should probably lie down."

I stood as well, hesitating, then leaned down and hugged Finn. "Thank you, Finn. I see why you're Una's hero."

He was stiff for a moment, then returned the gesture. "Thank you."

Upstairs, Niall showed me the adjoining room to his. I walked around, noting the feminine touches. I looked at him hesitantly.

"My mum's," he explained. "When she comes to visit, this is where she stays. Finn keeps it for her."

"Won't she mind my using it?"

"Not at all."

I sat down, my heart feeling heavy. "You want me out of your room, of course," I said, trying to sound light. "You need your space."

Before he could say anything, I laughed. It sounded forced even to my ears. "You must be tired of babysitting a silly woman."

He was in front of me instantly, gripping my hands. "You are not silly. You went through hell."

I shrugged, not meeting his eyes. He slid a hand under my chin. "Finn offered another room in the hotel. I wanted you closer."

"But gone," I whispered.

"Anna," he groaned.

"I get it, Niall."

"No, you don't." He stood, pacing. "You look at me like I'm some sort of hero, Anna. I'm not. I'm not a good guy. What I do is dangerous at times. For me. For those around me."

"I know that. It doesn't change what I feel."

He shook his head. "I think what you feel is hero worship. You're upset and confused. I'm safe."

"It's more," I insisted.

"You think that way because I kissed you. Your first real kiss. That will pass."

"What do you feel?" I asked, standing. "Pity?"

"No."

"What, then?"

He glared at me. "I'm attracted to you, Anna. I admit that. But I'm not what you're looking for. You deserve a house and kids. A husband who comes home every night and helps you tuck them into bed, then takes you to his bed and loves you properly."

"And you're not that guy?"

"No."

"Then why keep me close?"

He ran a hand through his hair. "I do care, just not the way you need. I can check on you here. If you want privacy, you can close the door. We can share a meal if you want."

"Like buddies?" I said sarcastically.

"I think with some distance and time, you'll see I'm right."

"I thought you felt it. You certainly felt as if you did the other night."

He drew in a deep breath. "You are beautiful. Sexy. You were in my bed. But I can't take that from you, Anna. It belongs to the man you give your heart to." He frowned. "Because, what I know of you, once you give your heart, it will be forever."

I blinked, refusing to cry. "Well, maybe the second time that happens, it will be true."

I brushed past him, stopping when he wrapped his hand around my arm. "Anna."

I faced him, suddenly angry. "What, Niall? What do you want me to say?"

"That you understand. This is for the best. You can stay here, be close, and I'll be there if you need me."

"Like a brother."

"A friend. I can't be more. I don't know how. Relationships and I—we don't mix. They always fail." He sucked in a deep breath. "I'm trying to be honest with you."

I dashed away the tears forming in my eyes. "Fine. When you decide to be honest with yourself, let me know."

"What do you mean by that?"

"There is something between us. I feel it. I don't have a lot of experience, but I feel it."

He tugged on his hair, then stepped close. "You want the truth? I want you. I want to kiss you. Hold you. Fuck you. Claim your first time. But that isn't mine to have."

"Why?"

"Because there would be no future. I would use you for a while, and we'd be done."

"Why are you saying that?"

"It's how I am!" He paced again, upset. "I'm not normal. I don't have the same heart, like Finn or Roman. I don't connect with people. I don't want the same things. I don't want a future."

"Who's asking you for one?"

He stopped in front of me. "That's who you are, Anna. You're a long-term commitment."

"Says who?"

"Me!" he roared. "I say so. And that is final," he added with a growl, stomping away, heading back to his suite.

I narrowed my eyes. "Then you're no better than them."

He turned at the door. "What did you say?"

I was so angry, I didn't choose my words. "They took my choices away. Made me a victim. Took away my thoughts and feelings. Now, you're doing the same thing." I raised my voice. "It's my right to choose. My life. My decision."

Silence descended, and I felt his anger. He closed the distance between us, and I stepped back until I was against the wall with nowhere else to go. He was furious, the rage rolling off him. He had pulled on his hair so much, it was all over the place, giving him a wild look. His eyes were narrow slits of black fury. His chest pumped, and his hands were fists at his sides.

I should be terrified. But I wasn't. It was Niall.

When he spoke, his voice was low and gravelly.

"I am nothing like them. I took you out of there and gave you back your freedom."

"But you're taking away my choices. Who I give myself to, who I want to be with, is my decision. Nobody else's."

"I. Am. Nothing. Like. Them," he growled.

I sighed, my anger gone and shame replacing it. "No, you're not. I shouldn't have said that. I'm sorry. But it's my decision."

He made a low noise, then exhaled.

"It's a huge decision, Anna. Life-changing."

"I know," I whispered.

The air around us grew heavy and hot. I ached with need. Want. Desire. For him. I had never experienced sensation the way I was at the moment. My body felt as if it were ready to burst into flames. Only Niall could douse the sparks.

Or set me on fire until there was nothing left but ash.

He rested his arm on the wall beside me, leaning down, his breath drifting over my skin when he spoke.

"And what is your decision?"

"You."

His breathing stuttered, but he leaned closer. "Even if it's only for now?"

I licked my lips, his gaze following the path of my tongue. "Yes."

Our gazes clashed, brown meeting brown. One determined and pleading. The other angry, yet a flicker of something else was visible. Acceptance. Desire.

With a low growl, he grabbed my neck, hauling me to his chest.

"I warned you. You will regret this."

Then he kissed me.

And I didn't care.

CHAPTER SEVEN
NIALL

I picked her up in my arms, carrying her back to the suite.

"There's a bed right there," she protested.

"I'm not fucking you in my mother's bed," I replied, my voice rough.

I felt her shiver.

In my room, I tossed her onto the bed, following her down, pinning her to the mattress with my body. We sank into the pillowy cushion, our mouths fused together.

I was angry. Furious, even. Turned on. Frightened.

I wanted her with a desperation I had never felt before.

I didn't want to hurt her. Physically or emotionally, and I feared I would do both.

But she refused to leave it or me alone.

So, I would give her what she wanted, and I prayed she still looked at me with the same sweet acceptance.

Kissing her was like air. Potent and life-affirming, and it filled me with euphoria. Her mouth was sweet and addictive. Kissing had never been high on my priority list, but with Anna, I could kiss her for hours. And I loved how bold she was right now. Kissing me back, licking into my mouth, digging her nails into my shoulders to keep me close. Her tongue slid along mine in sensuous passes, twining together, teasing, tasting, exploring. She nipped my bottom lip, swiping over it to ease the sting. I bit down on the juncture where shoulder met neck and left a mark. Then I went back to her mouth, holding her down, yet not pressing into her sore areas, all too aware of her still-healing injuries.

She seemed to have forgotten about them, dragging me close, wrapping her legs around my waist, pulling my hair. She tugged at my suit jacket, making angry little sounds of frustration. I sat up, shrugging it off and tossing it behind me somewhere. I did the same with my shirt and tie, not caring if the expensive cloth ended up creased, torn, or ruined. I gripped the bottom of her sweater, yanking on it, wanting it off. Wanting her bare to my eyes. She shimmied under me, pulling the garment over her head. Her breasts sprang free, and I captured them in my hands, caressing the already hard nipples. She whimpered as I pinched the pink tips, dropping my head to suck at them. She ran her hands over the planes of my chest, stroking my nipples, then down my torso, yanking on my belt. I slid away, standing by the bed, undoing the buckle and pushing down my pants and boxers, letting them fall to the floor. I kicked them off, my socks following, and I stood in front of her, naked, my cock erect, my chest pumping rapidly.

"Your turn, Polly."

That was the first time she hesitated. Her eyes were huge in her face as she took me in, gazing at me. I saw the fear and worry creep in. I knelt on the mattress, nuzzling her mouth. "I won't hurt you, *mo mhuirnín.*"

"I know," she replied, a quaver in her voice.

"Tell me," I demanded tenderly.

"You're so beautiful. So strong and fit. I'm covered in scars and bruises. You're a god, and I'm just..."

"Just?" I prompted.

"A pale ghost. Inexperienced. A body more like a child

than a grown-up. How could I compete with all the other women you've had? I don't know—"

I cut her off with my mouth, kissing her until she was breathless. I stood, tugging off her pants and socks, leaving her as exposed as I was.

"You are lovely," I murmured. "Pale, yes. Ghostly, no. You glow for me, Anna. Your skin is marked, showing you survived. Your bruises don't make you less beautiful to me. I want to kiss every one of them and watch as they fade every day until all I kiss is the velvet of your skin. And yes, you're tiny." I smiled as I looked at her, small on my large bed. "But not a child. Your breasts nestle perfectly in my hands. Your legs were exactly right wrapped around my waist. We are going to fit together so well."

I climbed over her, tracing my tongue along one bruise. "I'll start here and mark out a map. We'll count daily until there is nothing left to count. Nothing but skin for me to lick and kiss. Mark as mine."

I had no idea where my words were coming from. But they fell from my mouth before I could stop them, and at the moment, I didn't care.

She groaned as I started, caressing and kissing each mark. Every bruise. I traced some, nuzzled others, licked more. From her neck to her feet, I went, and then I started back up, pausing by her thighs. "I know where each one is now. But I think maybe you're aching elsewhere?" I ran a finger to her center, her gasp making me smile. "Here, *mo mhuirnín?* You're aching here for my mouth?"

"Niall," she whispered, grasping the comforter.

I sat back on my heels, looking at her. Committing her to memory. Her hair was spread over the navy sheets, a swath of gold on the blue. Her nipples were stiff and damp from my mouth, her lips swollen from mine. I wrapped my hands around her knees, opening her to me. She was pink and wet, her skin glistening. I licked my lips, stroking along her seam. She arched off the bed with a cry.

"Oh, very needy," I murmured.

"I've never. No one ever—" she babbled.

"I know, baby. That makes it even better."

Then I lowered my head, spread her wide, and kissed her clit.

ANNA

I hadn't expected to end up in bed with Niall this afternoon. Normally a quiet person, I knew the argument I started was unlike me. His reaction should have frightened me, but instead, it turned me on.

Because underneath the anger, his furious words, and his implied threats, was Niall. And I knew he would never hurt me.

And now with his mouth on my body and his tongue licking at me, I was a mass of quivering need and want. I had never experienced the sensations I was feeling right now. My own attempts never brought out anything like he was doing.

He groaned as he worked me, as if he was enjoying it as much as I was. He licked and sucked at my clit, teased my entrance, sliding in a long, hard finger. I gasped at the invasion, wondering how it would feel when he replaced it with his cock. His much larger, thicker cock.

He snaked one hand up my torso, pinching my nipple, then did the same to the other side. It felt so good, I cupped them as he removed his hand, pinching them myself.

"That's it, Anna. Play with them. Show me how much you like what I'm doing to you."

He cupped my ass, lifting me closer to his mouth, and I gasped at the added feeling. His tongue dipped inside me, twisting, plunging as he sucked on my clit. Pleasure built inside me, a slow, steady burn, and I rocked my hips against his mouth. He used one hand to hold me, the other to press his finger in again, adding a second and stretching me wide. He curled them, hitting something deep and mind-blowing. I cried out as an orgasm tore through me, obliterating everything else. I was a mass of responsiveness. Hot, cold, shaking, waves of euphoria crashed over me, leaving me breathless. He tempered his touch, his mouth now soft and gentle on me, easing me back to the mattress. He loomed over me, a dark shadow in the room, his lips glistening from me.

"Round one," he stated.

I laughed weakly. "More?" I asked.

"Oh, baby. So much more." He lowered himself down, and I felt his cock press against me. "I want you to come on my cock. I want to feel you wrapped around me."

"I want that too."

He reached over, holding up a condom.

"Do we need that? I mean, I've never, but I've been on birth control since I was in my teens."

95

He hesitated.

"I had bad periods," I explained. "And it's the shot, so I haven't missed any doses. I had one before I left to come here."

"Are you sure?" he asked. "It's been a long, long time for me."

"Really?"

He smiled, running a finger down my cheek. "Yes. Over two years."

"Then just you."

He tossed the condom away.

"Feck yes."

He bent his head, kissing me. I tasted myself on his mouth, finding it oddly erotic. In a move I didn't expect, he rolled so I was on top of him, holding me close, his mouth never leaving mine. My chest pressed into his, and I felt his hard nipples push into my skin. Remembering how he had explored me, touched me earlier, I sat up, looking down at him.

"I want to touch you."

His smile was wide, and he spread his arms. "Touch away."

I explored his torso, finding his muscles fascinating. They flexed and moved under my fingers. His biceps were bigger than my thighs, and he seemed to like it when I would run my nails over them. He groaned as I sucked his hard, flat nipples, and I liked the low noise he made in his throat when I dragged my fingers across his pelvis.

His legs were strong. Sinewy. Covered in a dusting of coarse hair like his chest. His feet were big like the rest of him and, as I discovered to my delight, ticklish. His bark of laughter made me giggle, and his threats about returning the favor made me roll my eyes. I wasn't ticklish in any fashion.

I swung my leg over his calves and stared at his erect cock. It was hard under my touch, yet the skin was surprisingly soft. The girth was astonishing, and I felt a flutter of nerves as I stroked it tentatively. Niall groaned, wrapping his hand around mine.

"Like this," he urged, showing me how to hold him, stroke him the way he liked. I ran my finger along the thick vein on the underside, my thumb rolling over the top, feeling the silky liquid gathering there.

I shimmied closer and bent, licking at the head. Niall arched off the bed, cursing.

"Feck."

I met his glittering eyes and saw the way he was fisting the comforter. I did it again, this time lowering my head and closing my mouth around him.

I was sure he growled.

I started to move, taking him a little deeper. I had no experience. No idea if I was doing this right. Except Niall was muttering, praising me. Then he buried his hand in my hair and begged me.

"More, Anna. Suck me harder."

I opened my mouth wider and sucked him in. I twisted my tongue around him as I lifted my head, then repeated the move. He hissed and groaned. Lifted his hips. I kept going, learning quickly what he liked.

Which, it seemed, was everything I tried.

Then he sat up. "Enough," he panted.

I frowned. "You didn't like it?"

"Baby, I loved it. But I want to be inside you when I come."

Then he wrapped his arm around my waist and rolled us. He kissed me, his tongue going deep as he fingered me again. I whimpered, opening to him, and he slipped between my legs. I could feel him, hard and thick, nudging at me. "Tell me you want this," he whispered.

I gripped his back, running my hand down and cupping his hard ass. "Yes. Make me yours, Niall."

He lifted his hips, guiding himself inside me. I gasped at the sensation of being filled. He stretched me, patient and slow, his movements controlled. He buried his face into my neck.

"Jesus," he whispered. "You're heaven."

"Please," I begged. "Niall, please."

He lifted his head, his intense gaze locking on mine. He eased back and snapped his hips, burying himself completely inside me. I cried out, his size too much. He stayed still, kissing my cheeks, his mouth chasing the tear that fell from my eye and into my hair. He murmured words I didn't understand, then drew back again, pushing back into me. This time, there was no pain, only a moment of pleasure. I gripped his shoulders. "More," I breathed.

He rocked into me. Long, unhurried strokes that made me whimper. He kissed me, his tongue mimicking his cock. I felt his hands everywhere. Stroking my back, grabbing my hips, fisting my hair. I wrapped my legs around him, holding him close. He started to move faster, his breathing becoming choppy. Harsh. He held me tight, his movements hitting nerves I didn't know existed.

My muscles fluttered around him. My heart began to soar. I started shaking, holding him close, crying out his name. He buried his head into my neck, groaning my name. "Anna, *mo mhuirnín*. Feck. Yes. Yes. *Yes.*"

I felt the heat of his release fill me. My orgasm was so powerful I couldn't speak. A long rush of air left my lungs as he collapsed on me, his weight pressing me down and only emphasizing the spasms my body was experiencing.

Until I was done. Sated. Adrift in a quiet fog of pleasure.

Niall withdrew, and I winced, already missing the feeling of him. He climbed from the bed, lifting me, and carried me to the shower. We stood under the spray, not speaking. The warm water felt good on my sore muscles. Strangely, I felt no embarrassment as he cleaned me, then himself, tossing the cloth to the corner, before wrapping me back in his arms and kissing me.

After, he dried me and carried me back to the bed, before sliding in himself and holding me tight.

I drifted, safe in his embrace, trying to gather the words I needed to say in my foggy mind. I sighed, tracing my finger down his forearm. "That didn't feel like fucking."

He tucked me closer. "It wasn't."

"Una was right. Your accent gets even heavier when you're passionate."

He chuckled. "Good to know."

"Thank you," I whispered.

He pressed a kiss to my head. "No. Thank you, *mo mhuirnín.*"

I was on the border of sleep when he spoke again.

"That was the greatest gift I've ever been given."

CHAPTER EIGHT
NIALL

I watched her sleep, for the first time peacefully. She was tucked close, her head nestled into my shoulder, her hand resting on my heart that was beating in a slow, steady rhythm.

I hadn't meant to take her to bed. To make her mine.

But I had—in every way.

I had never experienced anything as profound. Her trust. Her response. The way she made me feel. Not only physically. Emotionally, she stirred something in me I couldn't name.

I felt protective, almost feral, when it came to her. I wanted to make sure she was safe. Happy. I wanted her smiles and laughter. I wanted to be the one who made her smile and laugh. Every time she was out of my sight, I felt anxious.

I told myself it was because of the dire circumstances under which we met that made me feel so protective of her. Once she found her feet and life returned to normal, the need to watch over her would fade. She would find her life, and I would go back to mine.

Finn's right hand. Overseeing the hotel and casino. Handling problems and issues in his territory. That was my world, and I had no room for anything else.

Anna stirred, and I looked down at her, pushing away the hair that fell over her face. She was still asleep, her breathing deep and even. Between the news of Juan's death and our lovemaking, she was content and quiet in my arms.

Lovemaking. That was a new term for me. I hadn't had many relationships, and those I had been part of ended in disappointment, regret, and deception—and me questioning my choices. I'd stopped trying, my heart firmly removed, no one ever managing to reach over the walls I erected once I made my decision. After those failed attempts, I kept my relations strictly that.

Relations.

Dinner and a night or two. The occasional weekend. A gift—although, those were rare. A few rounds in bed and then I moved on. I was always honest, always open with the women I picked. They were clear on the rules, and I never strayed from them. If I felt they were wanting more, I walked away faster than usual.

And I never did repeats.

Anna muttered in her sleep, and I shifted, moving away. She frowned, nestling right back where she had been, her head in the crook of my neck—her personal favorite spot. I ran a finger down her cheek, unable to stop my smile as her lips pursed, and she nuzzled my skin, then stilled again.

I knew I should get up. Carry her to the room next door and tuck her in. Begin the distancing process. Draw the lines in the sand. Remind her she said herself she wasn't asking for a future. Only now.

Except with what we had shared not long ago, it felt too cold an action—even for me.

I'd let her sleep here tonight and tomorrow make it clear we needed to set boundaries.

Shutting my eyes, I tried to ignore the laughter in my head, the voice that whispered I had blown the chance of any boundaries by taking her. Claiming her as mine.

That voice could just feck off.

In the morning, I was awake and out of bed before Anna stirred. I lingered for a few moments, loath to leave her, but I made myself move away from her. I showered and ordered some breakfast, sitting at the table and sipping coffee so strong, it was midnight in color. The flavor was rich and robust. Exactly what I needed to brace myself for the day. For the conversation I needed to have with Anna.

I heard her moving around, and she joined me at the table. Her hair was damp and pulled back from her face, highlighting the delicate line of her throat.

She was unlike any other woman I had ever been with. My mum always called herself a "hearty Irish woman." She was fairly tall and sturdy. Her hair was a dark brown, her eyes a verdant green. All the women I had ever dated were much the same. Dark-haired. Taller, curvy. Sure of themselves and capable.

Anna was the exact opposite. Light-haired, dark-eyed, and short. She was quieter. Almost timid at times, although last night, she had shown me a flash of anger I hadn't expected.

I found myself marveling at how tiny she was, yet how well matched we had been last night. She fit me perfectly, her height and weight not an issue as I had wondered. I had enjoyed discovering every inch of her. And I wanted to explore her even more.

I shook my head at the odd thoughts.

"Morning," I greeted her, trying not to stare.

"Hello," she replied, sounding almost bashful.

"I got you tea."

"Thank you."

I studied her, making sure she didn't appear in pain. "How are you?" I asked quietly.

She looked up, our eyes meeting. Her gaze was shy, sweet, but calm. Peaceful. I saw no regret there, and I sighed in relief.

"I'm good."

Unable to resist, I lifted her hand and kissed it. "You're more than good." I nipped the end of a finger. "You were, are, *incredible*."

Her cheeks colored a little, but her gaze didn't falter. "Same to you."

I indicated the food on the table. "You should eat."

She pushed up the sleeve of her sweater before reaching for some toast. The top was a pretty pink color. She wore it over a flowered blouse and a pair of ivory pants. I frowned as I ate my eggs, searching my memory. She had never worn that outfit before. I glanced at her feet, seeing shoes that were definitely new.

"You look very pretty today. Did Una loan you some clothes?" I asked.

She looked down, swallowing her bite of toast. "No."

"Where did they come from?"

"The boutique downstairs. Apparently Finn insisted Una take me to get a few things."

I gripped my mug with more force than needed, some of the hot liquid sloshing over the top.

"Finn bought you that outfit?"

"I suppose. He and Una. She helped me pick it out. I said no, but she said Finn wanted to do it." She pinched the hem of the sweater between her fingers. "It's so soft. And she was right. I needed another outfit. I borrowed the dress I wore to the funeral, and otherwise, I only had the leggings and shirts you'd bought me. She told me I get a uniform once I start next week, so that helps."

I stood, flinging my napkin to the table, the conversation I planned on having with her no longer important. "I'll be right back. Finish your breakfast, and then we're going out."

"Out?" She frowned. "I was going to go visit with Una again. Where?"

"Shopping," I said as I walked out the door.

I found Finn in the office. He looked up as I walked in.

"You need me for the next while?" I asked through tight lips.

He sat back in his chair, an amused expression on his face. "I can do without you for a few hours. Why?"

I leaned on the desk, meeting his gaze, speaking slowly. "If Anna needs clothes, I will buy them."

He waved his hand. "It was a thank-you. Una mentioned she had loaned Anna a dress, and I realized how little she must have."

"And I will take care of it. Charge my card for the items you bought her yesterday."

"Don't be ridiculous."

"Charge. My. Card."

His lips twitched. "Am I allowed to offer you the same discount, or will you punch me out for it?" He indicated my fisted hand on his desk. "You wanna take a swing at me anyway?"

I narrowed my gaze. He was amused. His eyes were dancing, and he was relaxed.

"I don't care. But I pay for them."

"Noted." His grin became wider. "Una has decided she wants to sing this weekend. I'm inviting Roman, Aldo, and Luca, plus their better halves, to join us. And you and Anna." He paused. "You might want a new dress for her."

"I'll add it to the list."

"And I asked Una to marry me. I was hoping you would stand up for me."

I straightened. "What?"

He nodded, his good mood explained. "You heard me."

"She said yes?" I asked jokingly.

He laughed. "Surprisingly, there were no objections."

"Congratulations."

"You might want a new tux for the occasion. I think Una is going to ask Anna to stand up for her. She'll need a dress for that." He paused. "And we, *as a couple*, would like to purchase those items, as *our* thank-you."

I sat down and my shoulders slumped. "I apologize, Finn."

He looked at me. "You are such an *eegit*. It was a sweater and some pants, Niall."

"There was a blouse and a pair of shoes."

He started to laugh. "Is that what pushed you over the edge? The shoes? Una wanted to do something nice for her. I told her to take her to the boutique."

"I want to do something nice for her. After last night..." I trailed off. "I just want to do something nice."

"What happened last night?"

"Nothing," I lied.

He did the eyebrow trick, studied me, then let out a breath. "Oh. I see."

"None of your business."

"As long as Anna is okay. Una is very fond of her."

"She's fine. I'm taking her shopping."

"Okay, then. Have fun."

I stood to leave as there was a knock at the door. I went to open it, surprised to see Roman there. He carried a small bag. I stepped back, inviting him in.

He greeted us both, then turned to me. "At the risk of being punched in the face, I came to see Anna, then thought better of it. My wife likes my nose where it is."

I rolled my eyes. "What do you need to see Anna for?"

He handed me the bag. "When we raided the lab, there was a sack of purses in a room by the door. One of the men had the foresight to grab the bag, thinking they probably belonged to those held captive. Anna's purse was one of them."

I looked inside the small brown bag. There was a wallet, still holding a few dollars plus a debit card and her ID. Her passport was tucked into another pocket.

"She was talking about that with Una yesterday," Finn said. "Unsure how to even start replacing all that. Good call by your man, Roman."

"He took it last minute. Effie helped me sort through them. This one was at the bottom." He paused. "A lot of them have been returned. The rest, we have turned over to our contact at the police. They can check missing persons records and the like."

For a moment, I was silent, thinking of what could have been. Anna could have been one of those people. I exchanged a glance with Finn, knowing he was thinking the same thing.

I shook Roman's hand. "Thanks. I know she'll appreciate it."

"How is she?" he asked.

"Doing well. She is going to start working here next week. And she'll stay here for a while as well."

He grinned. "A while or permanently?"

I glared at him. "Whatever she decides she wants."

He nodded, tapping his chin. "You can tell her she would always be welcome at the Maple if she isn't happy working here. She's smart and bright. I'd find her something."

I heard Finn's muffled, amused chuckle. I stepped in front of Roman.

"She won't need another place, Roman. You can take your offer—"

Finn cleared his throat, and I rolled my shoulders, stepping back. "Thank you, but it won't be needed. Thanks again for this."

I strode away, letting the door slam shut behind me.

I heard the burst of laughter as I walked away.

"Feckers," I muttered. "Both of them."

Anna was delighted when I gave her the purse. I explained Roman had brought it, and she clutched it to her chest.

"I need to say thank you."

"Ah, he left already. He was on his way to a meeting."

"Oh." She frowned.

"But he and his wife will be here Friday. Una is singing."

"I will thank him then."

I glanced at my phone. "The car is here."

I escorted her to the elevator, and she turned to me.

"I should make him something."

"Pardon me?"

"Bake him cookies or something."

"I don't think Roman likes cookies."

She looked confused. "Why would you say that?"

"He doesn't seem the type. A thank-you is sufficient."

We crossed the lobby, and I opened the car door for her, sliding in once she was settled.

"I like cookies."

She turned from looking out the window. "What?"

"I like cookies. If you feel like baking, the kitchen in the hotel is fully equipped. I can get you anything you need."

"I see. But you don't want me making Roman cookies."

I wrapped my arm around her, pulling her close. She gazed up at me, her eyes dancing.

"No, I don't."

She cupped my cheek, her fingers soft on my skin. "Okay, then. A thank-you for Roman and cookies for you."

I couldn't help it. I kissed her.

And I didn't stop until we got to the mall.

CHAPTER NINE
NIALL

"I don't need all this," Anna murmured, looking at the hangers in front of her.

"You need clothes. I'm buying you clothes."

She laid a hand on my arm. "A few things. I agreed to a few things."

"That's what this is."

I had brought her to a store I liked to shop in. I had called ahead, and my personal shopper, Liz, met us at the door, seemingly pleased to be headed to the women's section for a change. After a few moments, she suggested that Anna look around, then told me she thought Anna was uncomfortable. "Let her look so I can understand her likes," she murmured. "I won't be far away."

I walked behind Anna, pulling a wardrobe rack. I found myself watching her closely. I figured out quickly when she liked something. Her eyes would widen with excitement, and that dimple I adored appeared briefly. But most of the time, she would walk past, and it took me a moment to realize she was checking out the price. After that, I simply hung the garment on the rack. Liz swapped out the rack, placing it in a dressing room for us. She checked out the items and added a few more. I added some I liked as well.

Anna looked shy as we walked through the lingerie department, so I decided which items I would enjoy ripping off her the most and added those.

At some point while we shopped, I had accepted the fact that my plans had gone awry and I was giving in. She wouldn't be going to my mum's room. She was staying with me—at least for now. What the future held, I had no idea, but right now, I wasn't letting her go.

"This is more than my entire wardrobe back home. Certainly more than what was in my case." She frowned, a small wrinkle appearing on her forehead. "I didn't pick all of this."

"I did. Or Liz."

"I can buy some of my own clothing when I get my first check."

I looked around the store, then backed her into the wall of the dressing room, shutting the door behind me.

"I want to buy you clothes," I murmured against her mouth. "And you're going to let me. Then later, you're going to bake me cookies and model your new outfits."

"And then?" she whispered, her breath washing over my face.

"Then I'm going to peel them off and let you try on another one. I might reward you if I particularly like one."

Her breathing picked up. "How?"

I dropped my head to her neck. "However you want, *mo mhuirnín*. My tongue, my hand, my cock." I nipped at her skin. "All three if you'd like."

She whimpered, and I dropped my hand to her thigh, skimming it over to her center and cupping her. I could feel her heat.

"You want me, Anna?"

"Yes."

"I want to take you right here," I confessed. "Hard, fast, quiet."

"You want to fuck me?" she replied.

I had been semi-hard walking behind her. Watching her hips sway. The way her mouth curved into a smile—remembering how that mouth felt wrapped around my cock. But hearing her say the word fuck did it. It sounded so dirty coming from her sweet mouth.

"Yes."

She met my gaze. "Do it."

I reached behind me, snapping the lock. She gazed at me, her eyes wide, a dusty, warm pink color infusing her cheeks and running down her neck.

Without a word, I knelt in front of her, taking off her shoes and sliding her pants down her legs. I buried my face into her core, inhaling.

"You smell so good, baby, and I can feel you. You want me as much as I want you."

She gripped my hair, tugging.

I rose to my feet, covering her mouth with mine. I slipped my fingers inside her underwear, stroking her, pleased to find her already wet. I played with her, pushing one, then two fingers inside her. She whimpered into my mouth, grasping at my shoulders. I felt her begin to come, tightening around my digits, her body shaking.

"Take off my belt," I mumbled against her lips.

She fumbled with the buckle and tugged down the zipper as I finger-fucked her into an orgasm. She gasped into my mouth as my pants fell to the floor, and I lifted her so her legs wrapped around my waist. Our eyes locked as I snapped my hips, burying myself inside her.

She shuddered as I started to move. There was no finesse, no buildup. I thrust in hard, fast rolls of my hips. She whimpered and shook in my arms. Her tongue played with mine, our breaths mingling, my groans and her pleas muffled and low. Part of me knew I shouldn't be doing this. She was still innocent. All of this was still so new to her. But she felt too good, and she was right there with me.

I felt her begin to tighten, and I moved faster, my own orgasm rolling over me like a tidal wave, sweeping me under and leaving me floundering. For a moment, I was adrift, then I realized the woman I was holding was trembling, her shoulders shaking.

I froze.

Feck. I had been hammering into her without a care. Had I hurt her? I pulled back, lifting her chin. But instead of the tears I expected, she was smiling. Holding a hand over her mouth to stop the soft giggles.

I felt my own mouth turn into a grin.

"Why are you laughing?" I asked. "You're hurting my ego."

"I'm pretty sure the woman in the changing room behind us knows exactly what we're doing. I don't think she appreciated your efforts," she whispered.

I grinned. "Jealous. Maybe I should offer—"

She slammed her hand over my mouth. "Don't even pretend to finish that sentence, Niall Black. I will end you."

My eyebrows shot up in surprise. It seemed my Anna was equally possessive of me.

We looked at each other for a moment. "Are you okay, Anna?"

She traced my mouth. "Perfect. I like fucking you."

I dropped my head to her neck. "Don't," I warned. "Just you saying that makes me hard, and I want to buy you clothes, not get kicked out."

Just then, a knock sounded at the door. "Is everything okay in there?" Liz asked, her annoyance mixed with amusement.

Anna's panicked gaze met mine. I kissed her then turned my head. "Great. We might need more items." I kissed Anna again, silencing her protests. "A lot more."

"Oh." Liz's annoyance disappeared at the thought of the commission she would be earning. "Let me know, and I'll get whatever you need, sir."

"Thank you."

Anna's eyes shot daggers at me. I grinned at her.

"Bring us everything."

Back at the hotel, I carried up some bags, Anna taking the rest. She had protested, fumed, and threatened, but I held my ground for the most part. I'd purchased clothing, lingerie, some dresses and shoes, as well as a new purse. And unbeknownst to her, I'd left instructions for other items to be delivered, when she'd seemed genuinely upset at my generosity and I thought she was going to refuse everything.

It was something else different about her. I was used to giving expensive gifts. Trinkets that meant nothing to me, except a transaction on my bank card. It never meant anything when the woman I gave it to wore it, cooed over it, or coveted the item. It was usually a gesture of goodbye, prompted by guilt.

Simply seeing Anna in an outfit I bought her gave me great satisfaction. Watching her delight over a soft sweater or a pretty pair of shoes that cost me less than a meal out most of the time warmed something inside me. The fact that she wanted to be independent was a turn-on, but it didn't stop this unknown desire of wanting to spoil her for the next while.

Upstairs, she unpacked the items, confused when I helped her hang things. "This is your closet," she protested. "Shouldn't I be hanging them next door?"

"No," I said with a shake of my head. I kissed her. "You're not sick of me yet."

She caught the back of my neck, holding me to her mouth. "What if I never am?"

All I could do was kiss her again.

She drew back, offering me a sad smile. Then she clapped her hands. "I need a grocery store."

I laughed. "I'll take you down to the kitchen, and you can get what you need for today. Later, you can order what you need online and get it delivered. I have to go see Finn and do some work."

"Okay. I might call Una. See if she wants to bake with me."

"Okay. If you leave the suite, take your phone."

"I will."

I paused, hesitating. "Anna," I began.

She frowned, looking anxious. "Yes?"

I had planned to remind her this was just now. Not forever. To assure her she would grow tired of me, or I her, and things would change. But the words wouldn't come, and I hated seeing her smile fall. So, I grinned.

"I like chocolate chip cookies. I prefer the term biscuits since that is what they are, but I like the ones with chocolate."

Her dimple popped as she grinned back. "Okay, then. Chocolate biscuits it is."

I winked. "Good plan."

ANNA

Una laughed as we pulled another cookie tray from the oven. The head chef had been more than generous when Niall explained what I wanted to do. All sorts of kitchen implements, all the ingredients I asked for, had been brought up to the suite right away. He also told me if I needed anything else simply to call, and he would send it up. Una had been thrilled at the idea of baking, and we got right to it. Soon, the suite smelled of chocolate and ginger. It seemed Finn's favorite cookies were dark ginger molasses, so we made a batch of each.

It felt good to feel normal. Baking with a friend. Laughing and chatting.

"Finn asked me to marry him," she confessed.

I clapped my hands together. "Of course you said yes?"

She nodded. "I did."

I hugged her, thrilled for her. She had talked so much about Finn when we were being held captive. She swore she would never leave him if she got out.

"I'm so happy for you!"

She smiled, brushing away a tear. "I'm so glad I got the chance to have him back," she murmured.

"I know." I rubbed her arm in sympathy. "We made it out," I said quietly. "Thanks to Finn, Niall, and their friends."

She nodded. "I'm being silly. They are happy tears."

I knew they partly were, but I understood her feeling grateful and the emotion that swelled on occasion after our ordeal.

"I want you to stand up for me," she said, looking hopeful.

"Me?" I asked, shocked.

"Yes."

"But you must have other, better, older friends," I protested, even though I was excited at the thought.

She shook her head. "A few friends." She paused, once again caught in the past. "We shared something no one else can understand, Anna. We have a bond I can't explain—even to Finn."

I understood. There were things I couldn't tell Niall. Things she hadn't shared with Finn. We knew and saw what had happened to the other. Heard the horrible threats and saw the pain they inflicted. The connection we shared was one that could never be severed.

"I would love to."

She hugged me this time, excited. "Finn is asking Niall, of course. So, you'll both be there."

The timer went off, and I pulled the final tray from the oven. "I think we've made enough."

She looked down at the piles of cookies with a satisfied sigh. "Finn will love this. I've been planning on outfitting his kitchen so I can cook once we're married. He's never used it except to make a coffee or heat something. Such a shame." She glanced around. "We should do the same here."

"I don't know how long I'll be using the kitchen," I said honestly. I was well aware of Niall's way of thinking. Even after what we shared last night, his views on relationships hadn't changed, even if he was spoiling me.

The shopping trip he'd taken me on was unexpected. Especially surprised that it was prompted by the fact that his friend—and cousin—had bought me an outfit. I didn't understand why he was so jealous if he didn't have the same feelings for me as I did for him. Maybe it was a male thing. I had said as much to Una after showing her the clothing Niall had bought me. She frowned but didn't reply.

"You're so sure he has no feelings for you?" she asked now, picking up a cookie and nibbling on it.

I nodded.

"Why?"

"He says so."

She laughed. "He also said you had to go to the room next door and then changed his mind. He goes mental when another man even smiles at you. Finn has always said how level-headed and calm Niall is. You have him acting crazy. Finn was sure he was going to punch him this morning over the clothing. Never mind the pissing contest he got into with Roman."

"Roman?" I asked, shocked at the idea of Niall acting crazy because of me.

She repeated what Finn told her about Roman's teasing offer.

I frowned. "It doesn't make sense. He told me he thinks the feelings I have for him are hero worship. Nothing more."

"Are they?"

I shrugged. "I've never had feelings like this before, so I don't know. Last night meant so much to me..." I trailed off when I realized what I had said. Una's eyes were wide.

"Last night?"

I bit my lip and nodded. "He, um, was my first."

She grabbed my arm. "Finn was mine."

"Really?"

"Yes."

I leaned on the counter with a sigh. "He treats me so well and is so protective. He calls me cute names, and I want to think I mean something other than someone he lusts after..." I ran a hand through my hair. "I don't know. If I push him, he shuts down. If I say too much, he gets mad. Then you tell me he's all possessive about other men." I shook my head. "I don't know."

"What names does he call you?"

"Oh, ah...well, Polly. For one"

"Polly?"

I told her about what he said, and she laughed. "Polly Pocket—that is cute. Finn calls me *mo chroí*. It means my heart."

"That's beautiful. Niall calls me little doll sometimes. *Mo mhuirnín,*" I said, hoping I was pronouncing it right.

Una stopped mid-bite of a cookie. "That doesn't mean little doll, Anna."

"What does it mean?"

Her smile was wide. "My darling. He calls you my darling. Hardly the term a man would use for a woman he wasn't serious about."

"Oh," I murmured, shocked. "He told me he thinks he's broken. That he doesn't connect with people—women —the same way Finn or Roman do. That he doesn't love."

She snorted. "Bullshit. Finn says he hides his feelings."

"Well, I can't force them."

The door opened, and the two men walked in. I felt my

heart race a little when I saw Niall. He smiled as he came forward, sniffing the air. "I smell cookies."

Finn laughed, walking to Una and pressing a kiss to her head. "What a great surprise. Niall didn't tell me what you two were up to." His eyes widened. "Are those ginger molasses?"

Una held out the plate, and he took one, biting down and closing his eyes. "Delicious," he muttered. "We need the kitchen outfitted ASAP."

Una laughed. "You want more cookies, my love?"

He grinned and pulled her to his chest, bending her over and kissing her soundly. "I want you pregnant and in the kitchen."

She laughed, throwing her arms around his neck. "Take me home and start then, Mr. O'Reilly."

Finn winked at me, bending and throwing Una over his shoulder. She gasped as he grabbed the plate of cookies. "Excuse us."

I laughed watching him stride to the door, carrying Una upside down, holding her in place with one hand, the other holding the cookies. At the door, he stopped and turned. "Niall, some assistance."

Chuckling, Niall opened the door and let them out, Una demanding to be put down, and Finn ignoring her.

Niall returned and picked up another cookie. "These are incredible."

"Thank you."

"Did you have a good afternoon?"

"Yes."

Suddenly, he crowded me against the counter. "Want to have an even better evening?"

My breath caught in my throat. "Yes."

He nuzzled my mouth. "Good. Let's start now."

CHAPTER TEN

ANNA

The next morning, I met Una downstairs. I insisted on going down myself. Niall wasn't happy, and we agreed on him taking the elevator to the lobby and staying put. I turned as I got out. "I'll see you later."

He frowned, glowering and unhappy. "You have your phone?"

"Yes."

"You know who the men are?"

I resisted rolling my eyes. "Yes."

"You'll—"

I cut him off with a shake of my head. "I'll kick your arse if you don't stop acting like a mother hen."

A grin pulled at his lips. "*Arse?*"

"It's catchy, you and your accent." I giggled. "You mix it up all the time. Feck, fuck. Idiot, eegit. You get more Irish."

He grabbed me around the waist and pulled me close. "Stop saying fuck," he hissed. "Or feck. You know what it does to me. You're going to get more Irish," he said with a leer.

I couldn't help my chuckle.

"I'm gonna catch you later and show you my arse." He pressed a kiss to my neck. "Maybe play with yours," he added in my ear, making me shiver.

"Stop it."

He nibbled on the skin, swirling his tongue along the same path. "And I'm not a hen. I'm a great big co—"

I covered his mouth, and he laughed behind it, kissing my palm.

Then he stepped back. "Later, Polly."

I was still laughing as I walked toward Una. I knew without a doubt he had watched me cross the lobby before stepping back into the elevator. That as soon as he got to the office, he would look at the monitor. I also knew Finn would have one focused on this area the whole time we were here.

I sat down after hugging Una. She looked better today, her bruises fading. Niall had kissed and counted every one of mine last night, insisting there was one fewer. Then he made sure by kissing them again. He was pleased and informed me they were disappearing under his magic mouth.

I couldn't disagree about the magic his lips and tongue could do.

I poured myself a tea, glancing at the laptop Una had on her lap. "What are you doing?"

She smiled. "Ordering kitchen stuff."

"Oh, fun."

She patted the seat beside her, and for the next while, we sipped tea as she ordered baking trays, bowls, and a new mixer. Measuring cups and spoons. Cute tea towels and oven mitts. We skipped over to the décor side, and she added a blanket and some toss cushions.

"For now," she explained. "It's so sterile."

I knew what she was saying. The only personality in Niall's suite was the navy-and-cream bedding. Other than that, it was exactly what it was meant to be. A hotel suite. A very luxurious one, but a suite, nonetheless.

I heard the tap, tap, tap of high heels on wood and glanced up to see a young woman heading our way.

She smiled as she approached, her dark hair gleaming under the lights. She was average height and slender, and she looked as if she'd stepped off a runway. She stopped across from us and dropped into a chair, crossing her shapely legs.

"Sorry to interrupt, ladies. I was hoping you could help me," she said, her voice having an odd cadence. Almost a singsong tone and slightly high-pitched.

"If we can," Una said cautiously.

"I'm staying in this lovely hotel," the stranger said, leaning forward. "My husband has been transferred here with his job, and I've come ahead to house hunt."

"I see," Una replied.

"Anyway, I am dying for some sushi, and the concierge said you might be able to give me the name of a local place." She winked. "He admitted he'd never eaten it."

The action drew my gaze to her eyes. They were a dark gray—unusual. Her makeup was flawless and done to draw attention to her unique eyes.

"Oh yes," Una said. "Joyful is just a block away. One of my favorites. Go out the front door and turn to the right. It's a fast walk."

"Oh, thank you!" Then she stuck out her hand. "I'm Heidi."

Una hesitated, then shook her hand. "Una."

"What a cool name."

She turned to me, holding her hand out again. "And you are?"

"Anna."

She sat back, looking delighted. "Una and Anna! What a great set of names for best friends!"

I tilted my head. "How do you know we're best friends?"

Heidi laughed. "I could see that immediately. You two are *sympatico*!" She blew a kiss into the air. The theatrical gesture made me laugh.

"How long are you staying?" Una asked, interested.

"Another ten days or so. I looked around with an agent yesterday to decide on the area. I love the waterfront. Queens Quay, I think it was called?"

"Yes. So, a condo?"

"Oh yes. I'm not into outdoor work, and neither is my husband. He is always too busy, so when he's home, we like to spend the time having fun, not cutting the grass. And he has always wanted a boat. So, it would be perfect." She stood.

"I'm starving." She paused. "I don't suppose I can persuade you ladies to come with me? I miss my husband, and I hate eating alone. My treat!"

We shook our heads. "Sorry, but we have plans."

She looked disappointed. "Another day, then."

Una nodded. "Sounds nice."

Heidi smiled and waved. "Okay, I'm off. I've taken up enough of your time. Thank you." She called over her shoulder. "Maybe I'll see you tomorrow!"

Una waved, and Heidi left, sailing through the front doors as if she owned the place.

"I wish I had that sort of confidence," I murmured.

"She is very sure of herself."

"I wonder what her husband does. She's about our age. Condos on Queen's Quay are pricey."

"They are. I'm sure she'll tell us all about it when we see her next time."

"No doubt."

Una laughed. "She is very friendly."

"She is," I mused. "Exotic-looking. And her voice is, ah, different."

Una giggled. "A bit of a ballbuster, I think."

"I think you're right. Lonely too," I added.

"I wonder if we'll run into her again," she murmured.

"I guess we'll see."

"Now, enough about her. Let's spend more of Finn's money."

I laughed. "Now there's a plan."

The next morning, I sat at the fireplace alone. Una would be joining me soon, but she was trying on some dresses for her show. Niall walked me to the spot, ensured I had some tea, and lingered until I rolled my eyes.

"I'm fine."

He bent and pressed a kiss to my head. "I know. Indulge me a little."

"I indulged you plenty last night."

He lifted my chin and kissed me. "You did."

I shivered as I thought about us last night. On the sofa, then against the wall. Finally, in his big bed. Everything he did, I liked. Every touch. Every caress. Every angle. Even when he gripped me, I felt his care.

It was never too tight. Never too much. And I knew if I ever felt scared, he would stop.

But I was certain that would never happen.

I hadn't asked him about the Irish term of endearment he used, or that Una had told me what it meant. Instead, my chest warmed a little more every time he uttered it.

"Call me if you need me," he instructed, kissing me one more time. I watched him stride across the lobby, chatting with a few people, then disappeared around the corner, heading to the elevator. I smiled to myself, wondering how long it would take him to check the monitor.

"Hi again!"

I glanced up, seeing the woman from yesterday. "Hello, Heidi."

"Oh, you remember me!" She looked pleased as she sat down across from me. Today, her hair was pulled back in a long ponytail, and once again, she was dressed to perfection and slightly intimidating. But her smile was friendly, and she seemed happy to see me.

"Of course."

She beamed. "My first friend here. Lovely!" Again, I noticed her odd voice. But I chuckled. She was very enthused.

140

"I wanted to say thanks to you. Joyful was incredible."

"Good. But it was Una who suggested it. She knows the area well."

"Oh. Does she live around here?"

"She works here," I said shortly, not wanting to divulge any more.

"Oh cool. This is a lovely hotel." She looked around. "Such a warm atmosphere."

"It is."

"Do you work here too? Is that how you know each other?"

I hesitated, not wanting to say too much. She was a little forward. "Yes."

"Work friends are the best. I met my bestie at work. I'm going to miss her."

"Where are you moving from?" I asked.

"Calgary."

"Ah."

A server arrived with a tray of tea for me. I smiled in thanks. Heidi eyed it with longing. "I love tea."

It felt wrong to pour myself a cup and not offer her

one. I did, and she took it, settling back in her chair. I searched for something to say.

"How was your condo hunting yesterday?"

"I saw a couple of places I liked. But my husband is particular. I sent him some pictures."

"I see."

"Where do you live? Close by?"

I took a sip of tea. I didn't want to tell her I lived here in the hotel. It felt too private. "Yes. A short walk away."

She nodded. "It seems the best way to get around here —on foot or public transport. Is it always this busy?"

I relaxed, realizing she was just making conversation. She was alone in the city. Missing her friend and husband. That was all. I needed to chill.

"I'm fairly new to the city, but yes, it is always busy."

"Maybe we can discover it together," she suggested. "Find our favorite coffee place and yoga studio, that sort of thing."

She saw my hesitation and frowned. It changed her features, making her almost ugly, but then she smoothed out her expression.

"Una can join us if you want."

"Um." I cleared my throat, suddenly anxious at the thought of stepping outside the hotel without Niall.

She shook her head. "Sorry. I'm being pushy. You and Una just seemed so nice." She stood. "Never mind."

I shook my head, feeling bad. "No. Sorry, it just caught me off guard. I'm a little shy around new people. Maybe we could do coffee next week."

"Oh, I'd love that." She looked around, then her eyes went wide. "Oh, my Realtor is outside. I'm late. I'll see you later."

She hurried away, and a moment later, Una and Finn appeared. She grinned at me. "Was that Chatty Cathy again?"

Finn frowned. "Who is that?"

"One of your guests. She's staying here and came over to chat with us yesterday."

"Room?" Finn asked.

Una frowned. "I didn't ask her that. She said her husband was transferred here, and she came ahead, looking for a place for them."

He frowned and pressed a kiss to her head. "Okay. I'll see you later."

He headed to the front desk, and I chuckled. "He is checking on her, isn't he?"

"Yep."

She looked at the cup on the tray. "She had tea?"

I nodded and told her what happened.

Una sighed. "Being alone in a new city is hard. I guess we can be nice. She is certainly vivacious."

Finn returned, handing Una a fresh cup. "Everything all right?" she asked.

He nodded. "Heidi Walters. Checked in three days ago. Extended booking. Suite. Credit card is in the same name."

"Go back to work, detective."

He chuckled and ran a hand down her head in a soft, intimate gesture. "Later, *mo chroí.*"

He left with a wink. I sighed as I sipped my tea. Una looked over. "Are you okay?"

"I'm good. I liked Heidi. I'm just..." I shrugged as I tried to explain.

Una patted my hand. "She seems nice, if a bit pushy. After what we went through, I think we're both a little leery of new people."

"The thought of leaving the hotel without Niall frightens me," I admitted.

"Again, understandable. But he and Finn will make sure we have men with us—discreetly, of course."

I sat back with a sigh. "Of course. I hadn't thought of that." I smiled at her, changing the subject. "Ready for tonight?"

"A bit anxious, but yes."

"You'll be amazing. Niall says you have the voice of an angel."

She looked pleased. "I love to sing."

"I can't carry a tune," I admitted. "It's terrible."

"I'm sure you're not that bad."

Unable to resist, I sang a few bars of a well-known song. Una's eyes widened, and she looked disturbed. I lifted my eyebrows as I waited for her reaction.

"Cookies might be your thing," she offered. "Singing isn't for everyone."

We both laughed, and it felt good. She wiped her eyes. "Oh, that was bad."

"And I was really trying."

She laughed again, then reached over and hugged me. "Oh, Anna," she murmured. "You are such a light for me."

I hugged her back. "So are you."

She smiled. "You are Niall's light too."

My smile faded. "I want to be."

She squeezed my hand. "You love him."

I looked over her shoulder, gathering my thoughts. "I think I do. But he insists he can't love."

"He will. Give him time." She smiled sadly. "Finn gave me time—he was incredibly patient and always there for me."

"He adores you."

She nodded. "And I him. Niall does love you. He simply doesn't know it yet. He will. I know it."

I looked down at my hands. I could only hope she was right.

CHAPTER ELEVEN
NIALL

I watched the woman walk away from Una and Anna with a frown. I didn't recognize her, although I was sure I had seen her in the lobby one day. She was probably a guest, but why was she talking to the girls?

Finn strolled in a few moments later, and I looked over at him. He joined me by the monitors, a small smile on his face as he observed them laughing together.

"What a bond they've formed," he said.

"I know."

"Fucking awful how it happened, but Una loves her."

"Anna feels the same. I like knowing she has a friend." I tapped the image I had frozen earlier. "Do we know her?"

He sat down. "Heidi Walters. A hotel guest. Apparently she asked the girls about a sushi place yesterday, and they chatted. Sat and had tea with Anna this morning."

"Anna never mentioned her."

"I checked her account. Everything seems normal." He grinned. "She asked William yesterday about a sushi place, and he sent her over to Una."

I laughed. William was one of our oldest employees, and, while very knowledgeable about the area, some of the newer fads didn't interest him. "I doubt sushi is a big item on William's list."

"Unless it comes with a plate of chips and some tartar sauce, no. I doubt raw fish ranks very highly." He picked up some papers. "Una made a list, but I don't think he could find it."

"Well, luckily, they were sitting close."

"I suppose so." Finn looked over some numbers. "Business is good."

I snorted. "That's an understatement. We're so deep in the black, we'll never see another color."

He grunted, looking over another file. "Everything quiet on the streets?"

"Yes. I checked in with all the senior men. Nothing untoward. No more fires, robberies, or areas of concern."

"That makes me happy."

"Me too."

He reached for the coffeepot, pouring himself a cup and taking a sip. "I'm going to give Una a ring tonight."

"About time."

He smirked. "I want to marry her as soon as she's ready."

"Of course."

"Which, if I have my way, will be in a few days. Not weeks. I plan to pull every string I have in order to make it happen."

I laughed. "Not surprised."

He sat back with a frown. "Roisin can't travel."

"No," I said with a shake of my head. "Not for a while." Understanding his line of thinking, I added, "She'll be sorry to miss the wedding, Finn, but she wouldn't want you to stop your plans."

"I was thinking of taking Una to Ireland for a few days. Visit Roisin. Let her have a party at the pub."

"She'd love that."

He paused, and I waved my hand. "I know what you're going to say. I'll stay here and run the show."

He frowned. "I want you to join us, but—"

I cut him off. "I know. With what happened, you've already asked too much of Roman. It's fine. You take Una and visit with Mum. I'll go after you get back. She'll see us both—just not at once."

He studied me. "And Anna?"

"What about her?"

"Will you take her to meet Roisin?"

I hesitated. "No."

"Why not?"

"Finn, we're not you and Una."

"No, you're not. Not yet anyway. Nothing is standing in your way—except you."

"I'm not relationship material."

"Funny, the past while, you've been exactly that."

"I'm helping her."

He met my gaze. "Bullshit. You're sleeping with her."

"That's not a relationship."

He took a sip of coffee, set it down, and held up his hand, ticking off his fingers.

"One, you refuse to let her leave your room. Two, you worry over her constantly and are as protective of her as I am of Una. Three, you buy her clothes. Four, you're ready to beat the shit out of anyone—including me—if they so much as look too long. Five, you're sleeping with her. You took her virginity."

I gaped at him. "You know that?"

"She and Una talk. About everything. Una fills me in."

"Jesus," I muttered. "That was personal."

He waved his hand. "It's all personal, Niall. This whole fecking thing is personal. And emotional. Why can't you admit you have feelings for this woman? She looks at you like you hung the moon, and frankly, you look back at her the same way. What the feck is stopping you?"

"I ruin every relationship I've tried to have. I just don't connect on the same level. It's as if there's a wall. I can't break it down."

"Maybe it's not you who needs to break it down. Maybe you simply need to allow it to happen."

I shook my head, and he leaned forward. "Don't you think I fucked up some relationships before Una? Jesus, I fucked up this one with her, and we found our way through, finally. We all have people we leave behind, Niall. We simply weren't ready for them."

I sighed. "I don't want to hurt her."

"But you are hurting her. You're hurting yourself too."

I stood and paced. "I keep thinking of my mistakes."

"Such as?"

"Marie—"

He cut me off. "Marie—you were infatuated with her fecking breasts and the way she dropped to her knees any time you were around. It was lust, you stupid feck. You were twenty-one."

I ran a hand through my hair. "I thought it was more."

"You grew up. Or, at least, I thought you did."

"I fucked things up with Joy."

Finn snorted. "Joy was a fecking adrenaline junkie. She liked being with you because of the danger you represented. Once she realized how boring you were, it was she who had an affair and walked. *Jaysus.*"

He was right about that one.

"I thought Tamara might be the one."

Finn rubbed his eyes, laughing. "Are you on drugs?

Tamara wanted your money. You figured that out. Fast, thank God."

"I haven't felt anything for anyone in a long time. I use them for sex when I get tired of my own hand, and that's it."

He dropped his head into his hands. "Fecking TMI, Niall. TMI." He looked up. "Are you honest with them?"

"Always."

He was quiet for a moment. "I met Una when she was eighteen. She left me with a lasting impression I could never shake. I tried to be with others, but my heart was never with them. It was always with her. For a long time, I thought there was something wrong with me too, but when I found her again, I knew that I had been waiting for her. My heart had belonged to her all that time." He blew out a deep breath. "Maybe you've just been waiting for Anna."

I stared at him, some of my doubts beginning to fall away.

He stood. "Stop blaming yourself for things you didn't cause. You aren't broken, Niall. Those women meant nothing. They weren't the right ones for you. There was nothing to them—no substance."

"Except I have a pattern. I pick the wrong ones."

"Then Anna is perfect. She picked you."

That stopped me.

"She is real," he insisted. "She has substance. A good heart. A loving heart. She wants nothing from you but your love. Why are you refusing to give her something you have in abundance?"

"I don't know if I love her."

He pinched the bridge of his nose. "Jesus, Mary, and Joseph, give me strength. You wanted to kill Roman for offering her a new start. Beat the crap out of me for buying her some clothes. You threatened Rodney. A seventy-four-year-old man with a wife of fifty-plus years and grandkids, for looking at her too much. Who has cataracts, by the way, so he can barely see. One suggestion of getting her a place of her own, and you shut it down. What the feck do you call it if you don't love her?"

I had no good answer.

"Let me ask you a question."

I nodded.

"If she were in an accident and you could rescue her, would you?"

"Of course," I snapped.

"If she were in the same accident with your mum, and you could only save one, which would it be?" he asked, watching me carefully.

I opened my mouth, but no words came out. I blinked, my heart thudding, my chest tight.

"If you could save them both but give up your own life, would you?"

"Yes," I replied instantly.

"Because you love both of them," he stated triumphantly.

I had to look down, grip the back of the chair, and take a deep breath.

Holy feck, was he right? Did I *love* Anna? The thought of her hurt killed me. The idea of her leaving was abhorrent to me. And I would trade my life for hers in an instant. Being with her made me feel things I had never experienced before. I felt lighter. Happier. As if the only thing in the world that mattered was right there.

I looked up, meeting Finn's knowing gaze.

"The lightbulb finally went off," he stated, triumphant.

I walked toward him, and he held out his hand, expecting me to shake it.

Instead, I punched him in the gut.

He gasped, bending over.

"That's for putting me in a fecking impossible situation."

"It was hypothetical!"

"Fecker," I snarled.

He laughed between gasps of air.

"Go get your girl, if she'll still take you." He sat down. "You dumb feck."

I slammed the door behind me and headed to the elevator.

But I was smiling as I stepped in.

Anna came out of the bedroom, looking nervous. I stared at her, enraptured by her simple beauty. Her makeup was light, mostly covering the fading marks, but she had played up her dark eyes and they looked huge in her face, set off by her long lashes. Her mouth was pouty with some pink stuff on her lips I wanted to kiss off.

She wore a dress I'd picked. A swath of royal blue, the color suited her. With a deep neckline and gathered at the waist, it had long sleeves, a demure slit on one leg, and suited her to perfection. I knew she'd chosen it as it covered the still-darker bruises on her arms. Her hair was up to one side, tendrils hanging around her face. She was elegant and sexy.

"You take my breath away," I told her. "You are so beautiful, *mo mhuirnín.*"

Her eyes widened, and she looked away. I stepped closer, brushing my knuckles over her cheek.

"What?"

"That doesn't mean little doll."

"No," I agreed tenderly. "It means more." I paused. "You mean more."

She inhaled sharply.

"I need some time, Anna. To put it all into words. The right words." I tilted my head. "Can you give me a little more time?"

Her answer was breathless. "Yes."

I pressed a kiss to her soft mouth. "Thank you."

I slipped a small box out of my pocket. "I had this made. I had planned on asking you to wear it for added safety, but the truth is, I want you to wear it because it's from me."

She took the box, her hand trembling. As she opened the lid, her gaze flew to mine, then back. I reached in, pulling out the bracelet. It was white gold, the banding a simple weave, the tiny chocolate and white diamonds woven on the top twinkling under the lights. It was delicate yet strong—like her.

"Niall," she breathed.

"I hope you'll indulge my choice. The chocolate diamonds are like your eyes. Brilliant and beautiful."

The eyes I was referring to sparkled at me as she nodded.

"This," I said, slipping it on her wrist and tightening it, "is called a bolo slide. Very common. But it contains a small tracking device. Undetectable. I'll know where you are."

"It's so beautiful."

I smiled. "If you press and hold it once, it will send me an SOS, and I'll know you need me."

"How?"

"Press it."

She did as I requested, and immediately, my phone, watch, and laptop all lit up. "If anything happened, if you were scared or lost or needed me, I could find you."

I touched the slide. "If the tracker were somehow disabled, if you press and hold it twice, it sends a different signal. One that cannot be disabled."

"Oh. Wow."

"We don't know the range. It's something Evan's been working on."

At her questioning look, I explained. "He's part of our security team, and tech is his jam. He handles all our gadgets. Trackers, drones, surveillance. All that sort of stuff."

"I see," Anna murmured.

"But since you're not going far, it should be fine in the hotel or the grounds," I continued. "Plus, it's just a precaution. An extra measure to help you feel safer." I smiled with a shrug. "And make me feel better too."

She threw her arms around my neck and kissed me. I responded instantly, not caring about her gloss or anything else. Only tasting her. Holding her. Kissing her back until we were both breathless.

I drew back, touching her mouth. "I messed up your makeup."

Her dimple popped with the width of her smile. "I don't care."

I grinned. "Me either."

"Thank you. For the gift. The care that went into it."

I gazed down at her. "A life with me would need precautions like this, Anna. Always." I tightened my grip on her waist. "There would be dangers."

"I know. Una and I talked a lot about that in the, um, place. And again here. I'm not afraid."

I frowned. "You have to think about that. What you would give up."

"I'd rather think of what I would gain."

"Which is?"

"You."

I swept her into my arms again, kissing her with utter abandon. My alarm went off, and I pulled back. "We need to be in our seats in ten minutes."

She blinked. "I'll get my bag."

"You might want—" I tapped her mouth.

She grinned. "You too. Pink is not your color."

I laughed. "I'll remember that."

CHAPTER TWELVE
ANNA

Sitting beside Niall with a group of his friends, I felt euphoric. He hadn't said the words, but I felt his love. It was the way he looked at me. The warmth of his arm around my back. The way his fingers played with the ends of my hair. The intense way he watched me.

Looking around the table, I realized it was the same for all the men. Their wives beside them, the adoring glances. The possessive glares they gave anyone glancing toward their spouses too long. I had to laugh to myself when I realized it was the same for the women. Vi's glare could pierce armor. It obviously amused Aldo, who teased her often, pulling her close for a kiss.

I leaned back into Niall's warmth, feeling something I

had never experienced before. A sensation of belonging. To him. With these people.

I knew his life was dangerous. I also knew, without his world, I would be elsewhere, locked in pain and misery —if I were still breathing.

Their world didn't frighten me as much as the evil that existed outside of it. I had no doubt Niall would keep me safe. That he would do whatever it took to make me safe.

I glanced down at my bracelet, running my fingertip over the pretty diamonds. I had never owned a piece of jewelry so expensive. My mom's and dad's wedding bands were thin, and my dad's had a crack in it. They were up north in the small storage locker where I'd left some items I couldn't bear to part with when I'd sold the campground and the small house I'd grown up in. I had planned on shipping them to Toronto once I was settled. I frowned as I wondered what Niall would think of the odd pieces of furniture and the pictures I wanted to keep.

He leaned close, his voice low in my ear. "Whatever you're thinking of that is making you so sad, stop. We'll figure it out." He squeezed my shoulder. "Just enjoy the night, *mo mhuirnín.*"

Una's voice was spectacular. I had heard her sing— soft and low on occasion. But hearing her, seeing her, in the small spotlight, I got goose bumps. She reached high notes I couldn't fathom as she sang Celtic songs, her voice filling the room with a power and emotion that packed a punch. She was applauded and cheered, no one as loudly as Finn. His eyes shone with proud tears as he watched her.

She spoke little, bowing at the praise. It was during her last song that the tears came for me, unbidden and hot. It was the one she'd sung to her brother as he lay dying in her arms. The poignancy of that moment hit me fully, and I had to grasp Niall's hand. He tightened his arm around me. Finn leaned forward, anxious and emotional as she drew to a close, tears running down her cheeks. She seemed to falter a little, and he was out of his seat in an instant, springing up on stage and wrapping an arm around her waist, guiding her off amid the applause.

The lights brightened, and I looked around the table, seeing the same emotion reflected on everyone's faces. You could feel her pain as she sang, and the sensation brought out hidden hurts deep from your soul.

Effie wiped her eyes. "She was simply brilliant."

Roman tucked her close, pressing a kiss to her head but not saying a word.

Vi sniffled. "That was intense."

Aldo only nodded.

"She sang that to her brother as he passed," I whispered, my voice feeling thick in my throat.

"Oh God," Effie replied. "What a brave soul she is."

"She's braver than anyone knows," I said.

Effie smiled at me. "Except you."

Niall's grip on me tightened, and he pulled me so close I had to pat his hand to relax him enough to breathe. He hated thinking about what Una and I went through.

"We were brave together."

Roman lifted a glass. "To the brave women in our life."

The room emptied out except our group. Una was only singing one set tonight, and Finn had arranged for dinner to be served to us here in private after he'd had some alone time with Una.

A short while later, Una and Finn appeared. Una was smiling and calm. Finn beamed in happiness. She accepted all the hugs and accolades with grace, then sat next to me.

Our eyes met, and a silent conversation happened. Everyone around the table was quiet, and I knew I had to help break the ice.

"I dunno, Una. If I were your backup singer, we'd be a hit, I think."

Her lips quirked.

"I mean, I could liven up the numbers." I waggled my fingers. "Jazz hands included."

She began to smile.

"I gave her a private performance this morning," I informed the table.

Una bit her lip. "I thought there was a cat in heat, but it was Anna, um, *singing*." She pulled a face. "Sort of."

I couldn't help but laugh. "We call it caterwauling, I'll have you know."

Una threw her arms around my neck, laughing. "Thank you," she whispered.

Everyone else smiled, and Finn met my eyes with a droll wink.

Then he clapped his hands. "Boys, it's time for me to show you the best of Irish food. You'll never go back to pasta."

That earned him some groans and eye rolls.

Niall looked at me and pulled me close, his voice low and gravelly in my ear. "If you're in heat, Anna, I can put out that fire later."

I cupped his face and kissed him.

"I look forward to it, you mother hen."

He had an amused glint in his eye. "I told you—"

I grinned as I covered his mouth. "Sorry. You big rooster."

Then he was laughing too.

I was curled up by the waterfall the next morning, enjoying the quiet. It was still early, and guests weren't up yet, the lobby fairly empty. Niall was upstairs with Finn, doing whatever they did. Hotel business, casino problems, his other...interests. I didn't want to ask or delve too deeply.

Una appeared, looking radiant. She hugged me, then sat down, reaching for the teapot. I gasped as the light caught the ring on her finger.

"Una!" I exclaimed, taking her hand. "That is gorgeous!"

She smiled, staring down at the large stone on her hand. "Finn said the emerald reminds him of my eyes. He gave it to me last night."

"It is exquisite."

She handed me my tea. "I know." Then she winked. "I

noticed something on your wrist last night." She lifted one eyebrow. "Something you want to share?"

I told her about Niall's confession. His quiet admission and asking for time. "This is a gift, but it has a tracker in it as well."

She nodded, tapping the infinity necklace she wore. "Finn added one to this after..." She trailed off. "Just in case." She grinned. "Our men take our safety seriously."

"Una," I asked, leaning forward. "Is it possible to love someone that quickly? Niall worries it is hero worship. I think it's more. He is beginning to think so as well..." I shrugged. "But I have never experienced anything like it."

She took a sip of tea, frowning as if in thought. "I met Finn when I had just turned eighteen. He shook my hand, and I felt something. Once during the evening, he tucked a piece of hair behind my ear, and it was as if he'd branded me as his. One touch. I loved him from that moment. So, do I believe love can happen fast? Yes. Do I believe Niall loves you and you him? Yes. How you met was under extraordinary circumstances, but you did meet. And you had the same connection as Finn and me. Instant. It's rare, but it happens."

I squeezed her hand. "Thanks."

We sipped our tea, enjoying the peaceful silence between us.

"Well, it's the dynamic duo!" Heidi sang, appearing around the corner. "What are you two up to today?"

She sat down, looking runway-ready as usual, her dark hair in a perfect braid.

Una smiled. "Not much. You?"

"I think I found a place my husband will love. I'm doing a second visit. Best part is that it's empty, so we would get possession right away."

"Congratulations," Una and I said at the same time, then began to laugh.

Una covered her mouth, and Heidi's eyes widened. "Wow. That ring is a stunner!"

Una glanced at her hand with a soft expression. "It is."

"So, you're getting married?"

"Yes."

"Well, we need a celebration lunch. A condo for me, a ring for you. You need to let me take you to lunch one day."

"Not necessary," Una said easily. "But maybe one day up in the pub."

"There's a wonderful bistro down the street," Heidi insisted. "You must get tired of eating here."

Una shrugged, noncommittal. "We both start work on Monday."

Heidi sighed and stood. "We'll figure out which day." She paused, her gaze on me. "Pretty bracelet. A gift from your beau?"

I only smiled.

"Isn't it just so *sweet*," she said. "Delicate."

I bristled at her tone, but before I could speak, Una did. "Anna is pretty tiny. A big bracelet like yours would look ridiculous on her."

I looked at her, seeing she was as put off by Heidi's tone as I was.

"Oh. Of course," Heidi said. "That wasn't a dig. I think it's lovely. Romantic."

"Niall is very romantic with Anna," Una informed her. "He adores her."

A strange expression crossed Heidi's face. "Who doesn't? Oh, I must go. My driver is here. Later, ladies!"

She hurried away, and I turned to Una. "Well."

"Seriously," she muttered. "She was insulting you."

MELANIE MORELAND

"I think, to her, this is a plaything."

"She's a plaything," Una retorted. "Bigger isn't always better." Then a grin pulled at her lips. "At least in jewelry."

We shared an amused look.

"She's a bit nosy," I admitted. "It bothers me." I studied Una. "You don't like her?"

"No, I do—I think. There's just something…" Una shrugged. "I can't explain it."

"I know. I feel it too at times, then wonder if I'm being too…" I trailed off.

Una nodded in understanding. Strangers made us both a little jumpy. Even seemingly friendly ones.

"She'll be gone soon if she and her husband are buying the condo. You won't have to see her again," I offered. "Neither of us will."

"Then let's not worry about it," Una said, sounding relieved.

"Good plan," I replied.

Una looked around. "I'm going for a run tomorrow." She pointed to the window. "Outside. I'm tired of running on the treadmill."

I lifted my eyebrows. "Does Finn know that?"

She grinned. "I told him this morning."

"And?"

"He pulled his hair, beat his chest, and gave me the whole no-you-are-not speech."

"To which you said?"

"Nothing. I kept drinking my tea."

I couldn't help smiling. "And then?"

"He paced and muttered. I think he might have called me something rude in Irish, but I'm not fluent. Then he informed me two men would accompany me. And only if it was in the park on the path and I didn't deviate."

"Which is where you planned to run all along."

"Yes."

"I should take up running," I said with a frown. "Except I hate it. I like yoga and walking."

"We could power walk together."

"By walking, I meant a stroll. Maybe with a coffee."

Una giggled. "You are so much fun. I could do that."

"One day," I hedged.

"No. Next week, you start work. When our shift is over, we walk. Goals. Those are our goals."

"But you'll be upstairs."

She shook her head. "No, I discussed that with Finn as well. I'm going to stick to the front desk, where you'll be."

"You don't have to do that, Una," I protested, touched.

"It makes sense. You'll be comfortable. The boys can track us in one place and not worry. Besides, I'll be leaving to get married and going to Ireland with Finn. It's not fair to start training, only to leave after a few days. Cleo in the front office agreed when I spoke with her earlier, and even Finn said it made sense."

"So, we'll work together?" I asked, delighted.

"Yes." She winked. "But I'm tough."

Grinning, I sat back. "Bring it on."

Sunday night, I couldn't sleep. Tomorrow loomed, and while the thought of learning and being useful was exciting, the thought of being out of the suite and involved with people again felt daunting. Not to mention the walk we were going on after our shift.

Una's run had gone well, although I had laughed when I'd seen Finn was the one escorting her. He insisted he enjoyed running and had been missing it as well, even as beside him, Una rolled her eyes. Earlier today, Tom and John escorted her, Finn appearing, trying to look casual as he waited for her return. Niall was sitting next to me and chuckled, and the two of them traded insults in Irish. Una looked between them, patting a sheen of sweat off her brow.

"You—" she pointed at Niall "—are no better. She is safe in the hotel. I am safe running. You said so yourself."

"Safe from any danger we currently know of," Finn stated smoothly. "We will always err on the side of caution."

She muttered something that sounded like "Feck's sake," and I chuckled.

"Careful, Una. Hanging with these two, you're sounding more like them every day."

Niall laughed and pulled me close. "You will too. Besides, I think you have a little Irish in you somewhere." He winked. "I know so 'cause I put it there."

I rested my head on the window, staring over the city, the thoughts of earlier making me smile.

I heard his footsteps, then felt Niall's warmth behind me, drawing me into his arms.

"Why did I wake up to a cold bed, *mo mhuirnín?* You should be beside me, sleeping."

I shrugged.

"Nervous about the morning?" he guessed.

"A little."

He met my eyes in the glass. "Say the word, I'll put it off."

"No, I want to. I'm just overreacting."

He frowned. "No, you're not." He turned me in his arms, lifting my chin and making me meet his intense gaze. "You went through hell, and this is part of healing. I know you're scared. But I am so proud of you simply for trying. If you're not ready, there's no shame."

"It's not that as much..." I trailed off.

"As?" he prompted, his voice gentle.

"I'm worried about the walk," I blurted. "Of going outside these walls where you see me and I'm safe. Even with men following us."

He bent and kissed me. Soft, tender brushes of his mouth. "Would it make you feel better if you knew it was me coming with you? Finn and I were planning on coming for the walk." He touched the end of my nose in an affectionate gesture. "I'm not ready for you to go out of the hotel without me either."

I flung my arms around his neck, burrowing into him. He was always so solid. So safe and warm. I felt protected in his embrace, as if nothing could harm me while he was there.

"Will I ever be?" I asked.

"Yes. I promise."

He bent, lifting me off my feet. "But for now, Polly Pocket, I'm taking you back to bed. Tomorrow, you'll take it one new task at a time. One minute, one hour. And all you have to do is press the toggle on your bracelet, and I'll be right there."

I laid my head on his chest. "Okay."

CHAPTER THIRTEEN
NIALL

I walked Anna to the desk, smiling at her, hoping to relieve some of her nerves. She was dressed in the hotel uniform, the colors suiting her. She had chosen the slim black pants and long-sleeved blouse with a waistcoat. She still got chilled easily, so she carried a heavy sweater with her, the cream of it setting off the blue and green of the tartan on her outfit.

Una was waiting with George, and the lobby was quiet, the guests mostly still asleep or at breakfast.

I tapped Anna's wrist as I leaned down, my lips close to her ear. "Right here, *mo mhuirnín*. Right here."

She nodded and walked away, greeting George and Una. Una glanced my way and tilted her chin as if reassuring me. I headed to the elevator, fighting the urge to stay and be close to Anna. In some ways, this was as hard for me as it was for her.

In the office, Finn waited, handing me a coffee. He'd set up the monitors so the middle ones formed a larger picture, zoomed in on the front desk. He didn't tease or make any comments since he knew exactly how I was feeling. I drank my coffee, and we started on our usual day, focusing on numbers and reports. Tasks to be done, areas needing visits. Shipments.

As the morning progressed, my shoulders loosened. Every time I looked up, Anna was smiling. Greeting customers as if she'd been there all her life. She and Una were often side by side, their heads pressed together as Una showed her something. I saw high fives and laughter.

"She's a natural," Finn observed, watching her with a guest. "Una texted me and said she caught on to the system right away. She's doing check-ins and -outs herself already."

"She's intelligent."

A woman walked up to the desk, talking to the girls. I studied her. "Is she a problem?"

He shook his head. "Overly friendly, from what Una says. She finds her a little pushy at times."

"Anna hasn't said much about her, except she invited her to lunch more than once."

"I gather she sees them most days and chats."

"Ah." I looked at the screen. The woman was leaving, waving to the girls. I tapped the screen, following her. She walked out of the hotel and slid into the back seat of a dark sedan. I switched cameras, focusing on the driver. He was broad and wore a jacket. From what I could tell, he was dark-haired with a heavy beard. Glasses. He said something to his passenger and drove off. There was nothing amiss or suspicious.

"Maybe the chatting will stop now that they are working."

Finn nodded, frowning over a set of numbers. Then he flipped the screen and rubbed his eyes. "Roman and Luca want to meet to talk about a few things."

"When?"

"Friday."

"Okay. Anything in particular?"

"Just an update, I think. It's been a while since we talked about the regular things." He stood and clapped me on the shoulder. "It'll feel good to be back to normal. I'm starving. Let's get a sandwich."

I glanced at the screen one more time. "Sure."

ANNA

Una was a good teacher, and I caught on to the system easily. I observed her and George handle some checkouts and an early arriving guest, and then I stepped in and soon felt comfortable. George went into the office to do some reports, and Una showed me the phone system, how to print reports. She also did some work at the concierge area, leaving me alone at the front desk, and I was proud of myself for remaining calm and handling a few guests on my own. More than once, I glanced at the camera pointed my way, feeling better knowing that Niall was probably watching me.

"Hi!" the familiar singsong voice greeted me.

I glanced up from the manual I was studying, meeting Heidi's eyes.

"Hi," I replied.

"How's your day going?"

"Good. Yours?"

Una came back, smiling at her. "Hello, Heidi."

She grinned at Una. "Our offer was accepted, so we got the condo." She smiled. "You'll be rid of me soon."

"I'm happy for you," I murmured, while Una offered her congrats.

"Any chance of an early lunch?"

I shook my head. "We only get half an hour," I fibbed. I simply couldn't bear the thought of leaving the hotel for lunch *and* a walk later. It was simply too much.

A strange look crossed her face, and for a moment, I thought I saw a flash of anger, but she only shrugged. "Okay. I'm going to grab something and head to the lawyer to sign some paperwork."

She waved as she walked away. Una looked at me. "We get an hour."

"I know. It was too much today, and besides, you don't like her."

"I don't dislike her. I don't know her."

I shrugged. "Tea and a sandwich by the fire is what I want."

"Oh, me too."

"Can we go together?"

"Yes. George and William help each other. Then you and I will do the same."

"Okay."

We finished at the front desk and went upstairs and changed. I tugged on my sleeves, trying to fight down my nerves. Niall would be there. So would Finn. No doubt a couple of men behind them. Or in front.

Maybe both.

I shook my head at my nerves. Juan was dead. I was safe.

I simply needed my imagination to remember those facts.

Niall came in, offering me a smile. He cupped my face and kissed me. "I hear you were a star today."

I smiled and nestled into his chest. "You always smell so good."

He laughed. "Are you trying to distract me?"

"No, just saying you smell good." It was true. He wore a cologne that had hints of fresh-cut grass and citrus —it was clean and rich and suited him.

He smiled and kissed me again. "Was it okay?"

"It was good."

"Ready for the next part?"

I paused. He leaned down, pulling a face. "A short walk. Then, I'll buy coffee. The fancy, foamy shite you like."

I started to laugh.

I pressed a kiss to his mouth. "*Eegit*."

He laughed. "Ah, the Irish is taking hold. I'll dose you up again later."

I moved away. "You'll have to catch me first."

His eyes gleamed. "Challenge accepted."

Niall's hand tightened on mine as we stepped out of the hotel. It was a nice day, although a bit cool. Perfect for a walk. I felt a tremor run through me as I stepped off the curb and crossed the street. Finn and Una were in front of us, their fingers entwined, walking at a good pace.

I drew in a deep breath as we entered the park. The air felt good on my face, crisp as I took it in. My hand was warm in Niall's. Around me were the sounds of nature. Birds chirping, the leaves rustling in the breeze. I could hear the muted noises of traffic around the park, but as we walked, it became more distant. I felt my shoulders relaxing, my tension easing away.

I was outside. I had always loved the outdoors, growing up the way I did, surrounded by nature. Working daily in the campground. I had forgotten how much I missed it.

Niall looked down at me. "All right, then?"

I beamed up at him, hugging his arm. "Great."

He wrapped his arm around my waist, tugging me close. "Great," he repeated.

We stopped for coffee, Una and I waiting at the table. I wasn't anxious or nervous, which surprised me, except I could see Tom not far away, and Niall was only steps from my vision.

"This is good," I said to Una.

"It is." She squeezed my fingers. "You have color in your cheeks, and your eyes are happy. I like seeing that."

"I forgot how much I like it outside."

"I'll help you remember."

"You're a good friend, Una."

"Back at you."

Niall sat beside me, sliding a coffee my way. "I added a shot of caramel."

I sipped it, enjoying the sweet treat.

We talked about the wedding, their trip, and their plans after. I knew they were staying in the hotel for the time being, and Una planned on learning even more about the business.

"What about after?" I asked.

"After?" she said.

"When it's time for kids. I know you said you wanted a family. Will you live in the hotel?"

Finn answered. "No. When we're ready, Una can have the house of her dreams." He paused. "Or the hotel of her dreams. I'll stay home and look after the wee ones."

She stared at him. "What?"

He shrugged. "Whatever you want, Una. If you're happy, I'm happy. You've always wanted your own hotel. If you still do, I'll make it happen."

She frowned. "And O'Reilly's?"

He looked at Niall. "I know the man to run it."

Niall stiffened beside me.

"Your, ah..." Una hesitated.

He wrapped an arm around her, pulling her close. "One day, we'll discuss all of it. What to leave, what to keep. What works with our life. Like Roman and Luca, there will come a day when we want to walk. To have a different life."

She gazed up at him. "Really?" she whispered.

"For you. For us. *Really*."

She buried her face in his chest, and he pressed a kiss to her head. I felt as if I had just witnessed an incredibly intimate promise between them. Niall tucked me closer, not saying anything, but I could sense his shock at Finn's words.

After a while, we got up and strolled back to the hotel. There was no rush, no great speed. We stopped on a footbridge, gazing into the water. Finn and Niall were looking up, discussing a huge nest in a tree, and I sidled up beside Una.

"Wow," I whispered.

She gazed back at me. "Wow is right."

"Did you know he was thinking that way?"

"Not a clue." Her gaze skittered toward the men. "Neither, I think, did Niall."

"You caught that too." I paused. "They need to talk."

"They will. They always do, in their own time. They have great respect for each other."

I nodded.

I had a feeling I needed to talk to Niall.

But we had to be alone.

I was already used to Niall and his comings and goings. I knew my life would never consist of a businessman leaving at eight and coming home at six. The suite always felt empty when he was gone, but I was comforted by the fact that he was in the building handling something. He had promised me to always let me know if he was doing anything else, and I trusted him to keep that promise.

I yawned and glanced up at the clock, seeing it was past ten. He'd been gone longer than usual this time, and I was tired. I got ready for bed, choosing one of Niall's shirts to wear since it smelled like him and made me feel better. I slid under the soft sheets, opening my book, deciding I would read for a bit.

Except, I woke up two hours later, still alone, my book beside me and the lamp on.

Worried, I slid from bed, hurrying to the living room to get my phone. I stopped in the low light, shocked to see Niall there, sitting in the chair, a glass of whiskey in his hands. He was hunched forward, his head bowed, looking as if the weight of the world were on his shoulders.

I rushed to him, dropping to my knees in front of him. "Niall, are you all right?" I whispered, my throat thick. "I waited and waited, but I fell asleep. What's wrong?"

He looked up, studying me. He reached out, running a finger down my cheek. "I'm sorry if I kept you waiting."

"As long as you're okay, it's fine." I cupped his cheek, and he leaned into my touch with a long sigh.

"*Are* you okay?"

He pressed his glass to my lips, and I took a small sip. I tried not to grimace as the dark whiskey slid down my throat. I wasn't much of a drinker, and he liked it neat. I found it strong, although I enjoyed its flavor when he pressed his tongue to mine.

He smiled and tossed back the rest of the whiskey, setting down his glass. He bent, wrapping his hands around my waist and lifting me to his lap. I straddled him, noting he seemed calm but upset. Or anxious? I wasn't sure. I cradled his face between my palms. "What is it, Niall?"

"I've kept you waiting in a different way. I've been holding back."

My heart rate picked up, my own nerves kicking in. "Holding back on what?"

"You." He paused, licking his lips. "Us."

"What about us?"

"I had a long talk with Finn tonight. He laid it all on the table. How he saw the future. His plans. What he wanted from me." He slid his hands along my thighs, reaching behind and gripping my ass. "He asked me what I wanted."

"And?"

"I want you, *mo mhuirnín*. My darling." He swallowed. "I love you."

"*Niall*," I whispered.

"Finn wants to walk away at some point. Maybe next year, maybe five years. But he wants to leave this behind. Enjoy life. Enjoy his family." His grip tightened. "I want that too."

"With me?"

"Yes. I want everything with you, Anna. Finn told me to look deep inside at what I wanted, and I could see it all. A house. Kids. Visits with Mum. Her bouncing the wee ones on her knee. Late nights. Vacations. Fights.

189

Making up. I saw it all like pictures. And every single image contained you."

Tears gathered in my eyes.

"The moment I held you, something shifted inside me. It was as if part of you slid inside my heart and stayed there. I've been fighting it. So fucking hard." He picked up my hand and kissed it. "I'm tired of fucking fighting it."

"Why did you fight?"

"Because I wasn't sure I could love anyone—not that way. There was always a disconnect. Something. And I picked the wrong women—the ones who said the right thing, acted the right way. And somehow, I always fucked it up." He gathered my hands in his. "But you are the right thing. The way you listen. Need me. Make me laugh. I feel complete with you, Anna." His gaze was so intense I couldn't look away. "I know I won't fuck it up, because this time, it's real. You're real." He swallowed. "And you won't let me."

"No," I agreed softly.

"I hate the way we had to meet, but I am so grateful it was me who was there. That from that hell, I found you. I can't stand the thought of not being with you. I want the life Finn does. And now, I can offer it to you. A life together." He swallowed. "If you want that."

"Niall," I replied, my voice trembling. "When you picked me up, everything went away. The pain, the terror. In your arms, I was safe. And the way you looked after me made me feel cared for. Loved." I slid one hand up his face, tracing his mouth. "You were so patient. So careful, so..."

"Inept?" he asked, pressing a kiss to my fingertip with a small smile.

"Wonderful. No one had ever cared for me the way you did. The way you do. I want to care the same way for you. I know you think it's hero worship, but it's not. I do think you're a hero. My hero. But I love the man he is even more."

He crashed his mouth to mine, kissing me. He tasted of whiskey and Niall. He felt like home as he wrapped his arms around me. He stood, carrying me to the bedroom, laying me down and following me to the mattress.

"I never want to come to bed without you beside me," he uttered. "Ever."

"Okay," I agreed easily. I slept well when he was with me. Nothing would harm me with him wrapped around me.

He tore off his clothes, then made short work of the shirt I was wearing by tearing it up the middle, the buttons scattering, hitting the floor and walls with small pings.

"I think that was an expensive shirt," I said, trying to sound serious. I loved the way he was looking at me. As if he was two seconds away from pouncing and ravishing me.

I was okay with that.

"I'll buy more. I'll buy everything you want."

"I just want you."

He lunged, covering me, his mouth hot and hungry. His hands were restless, traveling over my body, touching, caressing, teasing. He pushed my legs apart, settling between them as if he was meant to be there.

"We fit," he groaned. "We fit so well."

He was right. There was no height difference, no problem with my size. It was him and me. Our skin, our mouths, our bodies fusing together. I wrapped my legs around his waist, feeling him hard and scorching between my legs. Nudging my entrance. Then he rolled so I was on top, staring down at him.

"Ride me, Polly. I want to watch you take me."

I rolled my hips, and he groaned. He helped me, lifting me so I was over him. "Do it," he growled. "Take me."

I used his taut stomach as an anchor, bracing my hands on his solid torso as I lowered myself on his shaft. I trembled at the sensation of being full. Too full. He slid his fingers between us, teasing my clit. I whimpered at the pleasure and felt the rush of moisture that eased the final inches. When he was fully inside me, I hung my head, adjusting. His fingers gripped my hips, the shaking of his body telling me he was holding back. Then I began to move. The sensations were incredible. He hit some spot inside with each roll. Bumped my clit. I flung my head back, crying his name, moving, gasping, pleading. He arched his back, moving with me, the exquisite pleasure sharp but welcome. He grunted and panted, praising me.

"Look at you, mo mhuirnín. *So beautiful."*

He cupped my face, his thumbs stroking my skin in small circles. "My darling, mine."

He ran a hand down my sternum. "Feck, you are so hot. You feel so good."

"Strangle my cock. Take it all!" he shouted.

Every word, every movement, brought another wave of pleasure. Until it became too much. I cried out again, gripping my hair and whimpering his name as color burst behind my eyes and I spasmed, tightening around his cock and milking it. He sat up, encasing me in his arms as he climaxed, kissing me, our sweat-soaked skin sliding together, our tongues mating and entwining.

Then I collapsed against his chest. He relaxed back onto the pillows, holding me, his cock still inside as he stroked his fingers up and down my spine. I shut my eyes, the aftershocks rolling through my body, and he groaned.

"Every time you do that, it feels like you're hugging my cock."

"Well, I'm being friendly."

He chuckled and pressed a kiss to my head, holding me close.

"You promise me always, Anna?"

It was a promise I had no trouble making.

"Always."

CHAPTER FOURTEEN

ANNA

The next few days, life seemed almost normal. I was happy working, being useful. Being at the front desk no longer kept me awake at night. I felt the flutter of nerves at times, but all I had to do was glance up at the camera or touch my wrist, and the nerves would settle. Having Una there helped, and I grew more comfortable every day. I liked the staff, all of them friendly and helpful. No one looked down on me or seemed upset by the fact that I was being treated differently from other staff members in some instances. It wasn't better, but different. Few ever just started at the front desk. I asked Una about it one day while we were eating lunch.

"What would I be doing as part of the regular program?"

She chewed the bite of her sandwich, looking thoughtful. "When I first started at a different hotel, I had to learn from the ground up. I wanted to know everything, so I did everything. Housekeeping, laundry room, catering. I spent time in every department because I wanted to see how they worked." She took another bite, then grinned. "I doubt Niall plans on you running a hotel or being interested in the way the laundry is done."

"No."

"Some people are only trained on the front desk or the group desk. Reservations. You're not getting any special treatment, really." She grinned. "You're just watched over more carefully."

"We both are."

She nodded, finishing her sandwich. "Anyway, if you don't like the front desk, you can be trained elsewhere. Up in the office, accounting, wherever. If you plan on working."

"Of course I do."

"How does Niall feel about that? I'm pretty sure he doesn't plan on you working much."

"But I love working. Contributing. Niall's not a free ride."

"But he's a good one, am I right? Like Finn—all commanding but tender. I swear that man has some tricks up his sleeve."

I stared at her, and she winked and waggled her eyebrows. I started to laugh, and she joined me.

"What is so funny?" Heidi asked, sitting down across from us. "I could use a giggle."

Una and I shared a glance. Neither of us wanted to share our personal lives with someone we barely knew.

"Just something funny a guest said this morning," I said with a smile.

"Damn. I hoped it was dirty."

I blinked and she chuckled. "Just teasing."

"Where are you off to?" Una asked, looking at the case in Heidi's hand.

"Oh, to put some things in the new place."

Una frowned. "How did you get possession so fast?"

Heidi cleared her throat. "We rented it for the time period before closing. I wanted in right away, and the owner agreed. Odd, but it was what we wanted."

"Clever," Una mused.

"So, no lunch today since you two have already eaten. We really need to have lunch before I leave."

"Which is?" I asked.

"This weekend, I think." She stood. "Must get going. See you later!"

She departed, her dark hair swinging in a long wave down her back.

"I wish my hair cooperated like that," I murmured. "Hers is so perfect all the time."

Una hummed in agreement. "I can never get mine to behave." She paused. "Is it wrong I'll be glad to see her go?"

"She's not so bad. Just a bit pushy. I think she's lonely."

"I really don't want to go to lunch with her. The other day, she saw me here alone and sat down and talked for twenty minutes straight about herself. Her preferred brands. How wealthy she is. The car she drives."

"Maybe she was trying to impress you."

Una shrugged. "I don't care about that stuff. I tried to ask about her husband or where she went to school, and she clammed right up. Then she said she had to go."

"We don't like to talk about our personal lives either."

She sighed. "You're right. I guess she just rubs me the wrong way."

I patted her hand. "How are wedding plans coming?"

She brightened. "I think next week. Finn's pulled some strings and got the usual three-week window shortened. We signed everything last night. We were thinking next Friday on the terrace, just us and you and Niall. Dinner after. We'll leave for Ireland on the Monday."

"Sounds lovely."

She nodded. "I don't want big and complicated. I just want him. I know Roisin will have a party while we're there. And he thought we would host one when we get back."

"Sounds good."

"So, we need to get dresses."

"Okay. Any color?"

"Finn loves green. I think I'll stick with that."

"Sounds good."

"Things going well with you and Niall?"

I smiled widely. "Perfect."

She took my hand. "Good. You suit each other. Finn says he's never seen him happier."

"He's wonderful."

"So are you."

"Thanks, my friend."

On Friday, George finished a report he'd been working on and handed it to me. "Your time is almost up, Anna," he said kindly. "You look a bit tired. Take this to accounting and be done for the day."

"I have another half hour," I protested.

He patted my shoulder. "It is very quiet, and I am fine with Charlotte here."

I took the report, feeling grateful. I was a little tired. It was a rainy, dull day, and I had felt chilly and had put on one of the sweaters that came with the uniform. It was thick and warm, but the sleeves were too long. I rolled them up, but the wool kept getting caught on my bracelet and pulling it down. Finally, I gave up, leaving it tangled. I would fix it later. I was looking forward to going back to the suite, getting comfortable, and having some hot tea.

I loved this new addition to my life. I felt useful and back in control. But finding a new routine and learning so many new things was exhausting. I kept quiet because if Niall thought this was too much, he would make me stop, and I didn't want to. I was enjoying learning. Even meeting the new guests. Since I was surrounded by people and the men Niall and Finn had posted, it was a safe way to be with others and not be nervous.

I dropped the report off in the accounting office and chatted with the staff for a few moments, then headed toward the elevator. Niall was still out with Finn, and Una was working the later shift. She and Finn were getting married next week and would then head for Ireland, so today was her last day at the front desk. I would miss her, but I was excited for her as well.

I pushed the button, waiting for the elevator, when I heard my name being called. Heidi was walking toward me, smiling.

"Hello," I greeted her. "You look excited."

She nodded. "I was out picking furniture. I'm going to pack some more things and head to the condo to do a few measurements, then to the airport to pick up my husband."

"Oh, he's coming in today?"

"Yes. Just for the weekend to see the place. And me."

"Of course." She looked happy, and I felt bad for not going to lunch with her.

"You must be excited to get out of a hotel room and into your new home."

"You have no idea," she replied.

The door opened and we stepped on. She pressed the twelfth floor and clapped her hands. "Are you busy for a few moments?"

"Um, no?"

"I have a gift for you. I was going to bring it down later, but since we've run into each other, maybe you could come to my room and I can give it to you?"

"You didn't have to do that."

"Nonsense. You and Una have been so nice. I have a little something for her too. But I'd like to give you yours now if I could."

I felt a ripple of unease. I shook my head mentally. I was in the hotel. Surrounded by security. Niall could pinpoint my location at any moment. And it was only Heidi.

"Sure."

"Great." She dug in her purse, bringing out the keycard. "My room's a bit of a disaster," she confessed.

"I call it disorganized chaos. My husband calls it messy."

I laughed. "You must be looking forward to seeing him."

"I am glad this chapter of our life is closing," she replied. "I want to move forward with our plans."

It seemed like a strange answer, but I just nodded. We stepped off the elevator and headed to her room. She walked in, holding the door open for me. Inside, I felt my eyes widen. Clothes were strewn everywhere. Shoes lying around as if kicked off carelessly. I noticed all sorts of makeup containers on the dresser. Towels hung over the open bathroom door. A large suitcase sat on the floor, hard-sided and new-looking. It was empty and looked odd among the disarray. "You should let housekeeping clean up," I murmured.

"I don't like strangers in my room," she replied, searching for something on the dresser top. Her voice sounded different. Removed and cold, not the usual singsong voice I was used to hearing from her.

A flutter of nerves rolled through me. I looked around, not seeing anything amiss. Just an untidy room and clutter. I glanced back at the dresser, noticing the bottle of contact lens solution. Then the box of daily wear contacts. I squinted, trying to read the label. Colored lenses. Then I noticed something else. A wig lying on the floor as if forgotten and discarded. A long, braided dark-colored wig.

For some reason, my breathing picked up. The flutter became a torrent.

"Maybe you should give me and Una our gift together," I said, trying to control the sudden quaver in my voice. "We could do lunch tomorrow." I slid my hand over my wrist, finding the toggle on my bracelet. It was caught on my sweater, wrapped in the folds of wool. I tugged, trying to loosen it.

"No need, I found it," Heidi said, turning to me. Her usual smile wasn't in place. Her eyes, even with the colored lenses in them, were no longer friendly. They were cold. Angry.

"I really should go." The toggle slipped out of the heavy knit on my arm, and I turned it, trying to get it between my suddenly trembling fingers.

She smiled, nodding. "You're right. You are going to go."

Then she plunged a needle into my arm. "You're going far, far away."

The room began to spin, and I grabbed at the back of the chair to keep upright. I felt hot, unsteady, and dizzy. I stumbled and fell, my fingers reaching for my wrist.

But not fast enough.

Blackness closed in, and I was gone.

I woke, groggy, my head aching and my body protesting. It was pitch black and cold. I tried to lift my arms, but they were tied together at my back, pulling my shoulder blades together tightly, the muscles pinching. The air around me was hot and damp. I tried to stretch my legs, but I couldn't. Moving my head was impossible. I searched my foggy brain, trying to piece together the puzzle of the fragmented memories. It hit me all at once. Running into Heidi, her seemingly innocent request of giving me a gift. Her disastrous room.

The sudden awareness that somehow I had walked into a trap.

The needle plunging into my skin and the cold of whatever she injected me with running through my system.

Her furious eyes.

Falling.

The vague sensation of being moved. Shifted. Enclosed.

My eyes flew open in the dark.

The suitcase.

I scratched at the enclosure, feeling the slippery material underneath my skin.

She had stuffed me into the suitcase.

I opened my mouth and screamed. Then again.

There was only silence.

I shut my eyes again, forcing myself to calm. I could breathe—the air was stale and warm, but I wouldn't suffocate. But I needed to get out.

I twisted and tried to kick my legs. Tugged and jerked at whatever was holding my wrists, ignoring the sharp pain of the restraints. I pushed on the enclosure, trying to use my strength to break open the suitcase. Then I remembered it was hard-sided, and I stopped, panting and terrified.

Where was I?

Who the hell was Heidi?

Tears built in my eyes, and I stilled, needing to think.

My bracelet. Niall told me it had an undetectable tracker on it. And a backup. I tried to recall if I had managed to push the alarm button before Heidi had drugged me.

I wasn't sure. Could he already be looking for me? I prayed that he was.

I felt a wave of dizziness sweep over me, and I pressed my head into my chest.

I knew once he found out I was gone, he would search for me. Like Una's faith in Finn, I had absolute trust in Niall. He had come so far, admitting his feelings, confessing to his hopes of a future, that he wouldn't stop until I was safe. I need his over-the-top possessiveness now more than ever.

"Please, Niall, find me," I whispered. "I need you. I need you so much."

A noise made me fall silent. Footsteps approaching made me tense. They were heavy, measured. I had no idea where I was. If the suitcase I was trapped in was visible. If it was Niall, I needed to help in order to be found. I screamed his name. Begging. Pleading for him to find me.

"Niall! I'm here! Help me!" I cried out.

The footsteps stopped, and I felt the suitcase being shifted. The sound of the zipper sliding open was a low growl that seemed to fill the small, enclosed space I was trapped in. I felt the rush of cooler air hit me as the lid was thrown open. I opened my eyes and blinked in confusion.

The room around me was bright with hideous colors. Red, gold, purple, in blazing tints and textures. There was no rhyme or reason to it—just pattern after pattern thrown together, creating a dizzying kaleidoscope of hues. It made me woozy simply to look at it. I inhaled deeply, shifting my gaze and meeting the face of a woman—a stranger. I blinked.

Or was she?

Pale ice-blue eyes, like frost, met mine. A head of blond hair so light it was almost white surrounded a familiar face.

I had to lick my lips. "H-Heidi?" I asked.

She smirked, her expression frigid.

"The real me," she stated, her voice a lower register than I was used to.

"Please, don't do this. Whatever you want, Niall will give it to you."

She threw back her head and laughed, the sound sending chills down my back.

"Your doughy Irish man can't give me what I want." She smiled a cruel smile. "I like pain. Giving it. Taking it. I am so going to enjoy watching you be broken."

I started to hyperventilate.

She tilted her head. "Oh, I told you my husband was joining me. How rude of me not to introduce him." She stood, waving someone over. "And I lied a little. The gift wasn't for you. It was for him."

I dropped my gaze, unable to look. Not wanting to see who was there.

A figure stepped beside her, and my eyes widened in horror at what I saw. Red sneakers.

My focus dimmed, and I felt myself shaking. Whimpering. Struggling to get enough oxygen in my lungs.

Then he hunched down, and Juan's face came into view, his ugly, evil smile curling his lips.

"Welcome home," he said.

CHAPTER FIFTEEN

NIALL

I shifted in my seat, staring blankly out the car window, the scenery not registering. I was restless and edgy, a feeling I couldn't shake, no matter how hard I tried. It had started as Finn and I were meeting with some of his senior men, discussing areas and things that needed improvements. Finn looked after his territories, making sure they were kept up. Bad roads? Finn had them fixed. Trouble brewing with a new gang wanting to move into the turf? Finn had them removed. A family business failing? Finn made sure to send people their way. Many in the syndicate did the same in their regions, and it was easy to spot as you went through the city.

Last night, Anna had asked me why there were so many different groups in the syndicate. We were lying in bed, her head on my chest, simply talking. I loved being able to do that with her. I craved sharing, listening to her.

"Long ago, there was one 'family' that ran everything. But Toronto grew, and it got too big for one group to manage. There was too much infighting and a lot of problems. Things changed, and it was chopped into territories and different groups. It grew again. It's still growing. The syndicate has changed with newer, younger generations. It's evolved like the city. This generation is about peace. Maintaining control using different ways than the past," I explained. *"Finn is tough, but he wants to see his territories flourish. He takes care of them. They, in turn, are loyal."*

"And when they're not?" she asked.

"Then it is handled," I said firmly, not wanting her to ask more.

She was quiet, then spoke again. "And you're willing to leave it?"

"Absolutely. When Finn calls it, I'm with him. I'll run the hotel if that's what he wants. Or if he sells it, I'll find something else." I chuckled. *"Or retire and enjoy life."* I pressed a kiss to her head. *"With you."*

"Here or Ireland?"

I thought about it for a moment, running my fingers through her soft hair. The motion relaxed me, and she

*loved it. "Here. Ireland will forever be my homeland, but
this is where I found myself. We can buy a place there to
have when we visit, but this is my home now."*

*I tugged on her hair, and she lifted her head. I bent and
kissed her. "You are my home."*

*Her eyes shone with tears, and she pulled my head back,
kissing me deeply.*

There was no more conversation.

Finn clearing his throat brought me back to the
present. He frowned, looking at me and the way my
leg was bouncing up and down. "What is up with
you?"

"I have no idea. I have this odd sensation something is
wrong."

"With?"

I glanced at my phone. Anna's tracker blinked,
showing her in the hotel. Everything was fine with our
meetings. Positive and on track. But still, the pit of
anxiety in my stomach grew.

"I don't know."

I dialed Anna's phone, frowning when it went to voice
mail. I looked at Finn, who called Una. He spoke and
hung up. "She was tired, and George said she looked a

bit under the weather. She was cold all day. He sent her upstairs early, so she's probably lying down. Una will go check on her in a few moments—she's just waiting for George to come back."

That made me feel better. Anna wasn't a huge cell phone fan. She carried hers more to please me than anything. She had no apps, no games, nothing to keep her glued to the screen. She usually plugged it in by the sofa, refusing to take it into the bedroom at night. If she wasn't feeling well, no doubt she was napping and not hearing the phone ring. She probably forgot it in her purse—it wouldn't be the first time.

"Great."

"We'll be at the hotel in twenty minutes," Rory called over his shoulder.

I glanced down at the tracker again, confused. It had stopped blinking. It held steady, the light red not green. I refreshed it, the light still red.

I called our security team, demanding to speak to Evan, explaining what had happened. He was in charge of all our toys and was brilliant at it. He tapped on his keyboard. "It shows a malfunction," he muttered. "I don't understand. I'm putting you on speaker."

I looked at Finn. "I need Una upstairs now."

He called, and I heard him talking, listened to Evan typing. My heart began to race, the feeling of worry I had been experiencing turning into fear.

Evan spoke. "It's back online."

I breathed a sigh of relief until his next words. "It shows her somewhere, moving away from the hotel."

"What?"

Finn looked up, his expression worried. "Una says Anna isn't in your room. Her phone isn't there either."

"Rory! I need back to the hotel *now*!" I roared.

"On it," he replied, the sound of the engine revving high filling the car. "Ten minutes."

"The signal is gone again," Evan said. "I'm going to work on a different angle."

"I'll be there soon," I said through gritted teeth.

Across from me, Finn was speaking rapidly into his phone. "Get every camera searching for Anna. Load up all the images from two o'clock onward, starting from the front desk. We'll be in the security room shortly."

He hung up, meeting my gaze. His was focused, intense. "We'll find her. I'm sure there's an explanation." He spoke louder. "Whatever tickets we get for running reds, we'll pay, Rory. Step on it."

I swallowed down my panic. I knew what the explanation was.

Somehow, despite all our measures, she'd been taken.

And I needed to find her.

Fast.

ANNA

I blinked at the image of Juan in front of me. His evil smile.

"No. You're dead."

He shook his head. "No."

"But they found your body," I protested, as if by saying it out loud, it would be true.

He tutted. "They found *a* body."

He gripped my shoulders, pulling me from the suitcase. All my muscles screamed in pain at the rough handling and as the blood flow was restored to my bent limbs. He laughed, the sound making the hairs on my neck stand up. He pushed me into the wall, my hands still tied behind my back, the pins and needles unbearable. I shook with the aches already forming. I fought against the tears, but he saw them, and they delighted him.

He paced the room, talking. "Unlike my cocky uncle, I was wearing a vest. I was shot in the chest and shoulder, and there was enough blood they didn't even check. In the chaos, I slipped down the stairs, and I took one of the lab workers who had my build and coloring. I convinced him I would help him escape what was happening. We used another tunnel and came out not far from the barn." He held up his hands. "Then I gave him his reward. A bullet in the chest. A switch of shoes and clothes, some careful staging, and ta-da! Here I am." He tilted his head. "Did you miss me?"

"His-his hands," I stuttered.

"Ah yes. A dull saw, then I let Mother Nature help. Lots of coyotes around there. The blood would draw them. I knew I would be found." He winked. "Gave me time to call my wife and plan our next move."

Heidi watched from the chair, looking bored.

"I don't understand," I whispered. "Why didn't you run?"

"And leave you, my little pet, behind? Let someone else have you? No." He shook his head. "*No.*"

Heidi stood with a smirk. "My husband wanted you. So, I decided, like the good wife I am, to get you for him. I did the research on your Irishmen and came up with a plan." She looked at her nails, inspecting them. "That's what I do. I befriend people and let Juan have them." She narrowed her eyes. "You and your Una refused to let me befriend you. All I needed was to get you out of that hotel so Juan could have you. Your guards proved to be too close to let that happen. You refused to come to lunch. I couldn't fucking separate the two of you. So, we came up with a different plan. So simple." She eyed the suitcase on the floor. "I walked you right past them." She laughed in delight. "I even stopped by the front desk and spoke with Una on the way out. Your stupid men watched me load you into a trunk, and they had no idea. Not a clue the man helping me take you away was the man they were supposed to protect you from." She clapped her hands. "And now it's too late."

I swallowed, putting on a brave face. "Maybe not. Niall won't stop until he finds me."

"And how will he do that?" She held up my bracelet. "With this? I saw it as I was tying your hands, and I know your overly protective lover gave it to you. I put it in a blocking device in the car, and this room is protected, so it doesn't work if he put a tracker in it."

My heart sank.

She studied it. "Pretty thing. I think I'll keep it."

"No, it's mine."

She shook her head, looking at it. "I think it goes with my outfit." She tried to tug it over her wrist, but it was too small.

She yanked on it impatiently, and I got upset. "Stop it —you'll break it!" I pleaded. Then an idea struck. "I'll tell you how to open it. Just be careful with it."

"How?" she demanded.

I tamped down my nerves. "You have to press the toggle twice and hold it each time. It, ah, unlocks it."

She frowned, fussing with it. "It still didn't open!"

"Maybe it jammed when you took it off me. Try again."

She did, and nothing happened. In anger, she flung it at me, hitting me in the face with it, narrowly missing my eye. "Cheap piece of crap." She stormed away.

Juan watched her, somehow enjoying her irc. "You bruised my little doll."

I took a deep breath, my hopes soaring. Because as she flung it at me, I saw a small flash of light. I prayed it meant what I thought it did. That somehow my idea would work and Niall could find me.

The hope gave me courage.

"I am not your little doll," I spat.

He glared at me, strolling close and bending over to meet my eyes. "Your time away has made you bold." His eyes were cold and menacing as he crowded me into the wall. I refused to back down this time.

"Get used to it," I replied.

He slapped me, the sound of his hit loud in the room. Pain exploded in my cheek, and I had to shut my eyes and bite back my scream.

He was furious when I made no noise. He started yelling, screaming in my face, but I remained still, my eyes firmly shut, picturing Niall killing him. Slowly.

Juan pushed me down, dragging me over the rough carpet, the fibers biting into my bound arms and hands. He threw me into the closet, still screaming, slamming the door. I lay on the floor, panting and terrified, but the door remained shut. I could hear his curses fading, and I realized he had left the room, Heidi's voice trailing off as well as she followed him. I lifted my head, my cheek throbbing. Caught on my sweater was my bracelet. Ignoring the fresh agony that tore through my hands, I managed to struggle upright, and I used my teeth to grab the collar of my sweater, shaking the bracelet loose. I shifted and rolled, biting back my pain and wriggling on the floor until I felt the bracelet in my hand and I got the toggle where I needed it.

Then I started to press. Every few moments, I repeated it.

"Please, Niall. Hear me. Find me."

NIALL

I was out of the car before Rory brought it to a screeching halt. I raced to the elevator, Finn on my heels. In the security room, we were greeted with serious faces.

"What?" I demanded.

Evan clicked on the screen. "Watch."

I saw Anna leave the front desk and again as she left the accounting area and headed to the elevator. She looked up, greeting someone, and they got into the elevator. The feed switched, and I narrowed my eyes.

"It's that woman," I mumbled. "Heidi, I think."

"Yes."

The feeds switched again, and Anna walked down the hall to what I assumed was Heidi's room. They appeared to be chatting, and Anna looked relaxed. They walked in, and I glanced Evan's way. "What next?"

"Keep your eyes on the screen. There's a time jump."

Heidi walked out of the room, rolling a suitcase. She waited by the elevator, smiling at someone getting off on her floor then stepping in, and the door closed behind her.

"Where is Anna?" I asked.

Had she stayed in Heidi's room?

Evan didn't respond. He cut to the main floor, and I watched as Heidi stopped at the front desk, spoke with Una, then headed out the front door. A car waited, the same one as the other day, only this time, the driver got out and helped her stow the bag in the trunk. I frowned, staring at the screen. He still had a beard, but his hair wasn't long. And the suit jacket he wore was too big—he was much slimmer than I had originally thought.

Clarity hit me, and I turned to Evan.

"It was shortly before that when the signal died," he confirmed. "It came back as the car started to move, then disappeared again."

"She's in the suitcase," I said, stunned and horrified.

"They stuffed her in a suitcase and took her out of here with everyone watching."

Just then, the driver turned, faced the camera, and smiled.

And my blood ran cold.

"It's Juan!" I shouted. I turned to Finn. "He's fucking alive, and they got her."

Finn grabbed my shoulders.

"And we'll get her back." He shook me. "I fucking promise."

Around me was chaos. Evan was typing away, trying to find camera angles and search for the signal. Finn phoned Roman, telling him what happened.

"It's Juan," he muttered. "He's alive."

I heard Roman's shouted reply. "Jesus fucking Christ! We're on our way."

Una showed up, Finn telling her what we had discovered. She burst into tears, collapsing against his chest. He pulled her out of the room.

I was numb.

I promised Anna I would keep her safe. I insisted there was no better place than right here in this hotel. I had her watched. Finn had extra men.

And still, she was taken.

Simply the thought of how terrified she must be caused a chasm to split my chest in two. Knowing what a sick, twisted man Juan was, I was stagnant with fear. I watched the images on the screen over and over. My Anna, my darling, had been shoved into a suitcase and wheeled out of here like yesterday's soiled laundry heading to the cleaners. My anger began to boil inside me, the rage bringing me to my feet.

"Give me a job. Now."

Evan looked up just as it happened. My phone lit up. My watch vibrated. In my bag I had flung on the floor when I rushed in, a signal sounded from my laptop.

Anna's SOS.

"Holy shit, it's still working," Evan muttered, grabbing my phone. "It's weak."

"Can you locate it?"

"I'll try."

He sat down at the computer and started typing. Finn and Una came back, her red-eyed and Finn holding a sheet of paper.

"Una had a thought, Evan."

"What?" he asked, not looking up.

"When you check in, we require a cell number. I have hers—if it's real," Una said.

He held out his hand, and Finn gave him the paper. Evan turned to another colleague. "Ben, check this out."

Ben grabbed the paper, sitting down and typing fast.

Una came to me. "I'm sorry," she whispered. "She—Heidi—has been taking things to her new place. She said it was full of clothes. I never thought..." She trailed off with a sob.

I hugged her tight. "No one would have. This was planned, and she's been waiting."

"Anna was right there, and I didn't know," she cried.

I looked at Finn, shaking my head. "It's not your fault, Una," I assured her. "We're going to get her back. We've got backup coming—"

My phone and watch lit up again.

"Is that a malfunction?" I asked Evan.

It happened again.

Then again.

He looked up. "I'd say no. She's sending signals."

I shut my eyes. Signals were good. It meant she was alive.

"Hold on, *mo mhuirnín*," I thought. "We're coming. I promise."

Evan looked up. "I need room. And quiet."

Finn nodded. "We'll be in my office."

We headed downstairs, Una tucked into Finn's side, the occasional sob escaping her mouth. I was quiet, praying, desperately hoping.

In his office, Finn threw back a whiskey and handed me a glass. "You need this."

"How is he alive?" I muttered. "And who the hell is this Heidi to him?"

Finn rubbed his eyes. "He mustn't have been as hurt as we thought. He must have killed someone else and made it appear to be him. One of the lab workers, maybe. We didn't have an accurate count of them."

"Heidi never said her husband's name. Do you really think they're married?" Una asked.

"God knows. But she isn't who she said she was. I guarantee there's no condo or job transfer. She's been trying to get Anna out of the hotel the whole time." I stopped. "And you."

"Jesus," Finn breathed. *"Jesus."*

He grabbed Una and held her close.

"Today must have been Plan B. Or maybe it was the plan the whole time. I don't know." I scrubbed my face. "He was even more obsessed than we thought."

Evan walked in, heading straight to Finn's computer. "We hacked into a few systems and found her carrier. Then we hacked further into her account—"

I cut him off. "And?"

He sighed. "We located the area her phone is in. It matches with the area the tracker is pinging from." He turned the screen. "Look familiar?"

Finn and I stared at the screen.

"Holy shit."

Roman and Aldo walked in after Evan had stepped out, both of them serious and angry.

"Any update?"

"We think he's holding her at the racetrack."

Roman frowned, stroking his chin. "Good idea. Place is locked up, supposedly deserted."

"Power is still on for the security systems. We checked," Finn informed them.

Aldo leaned against the wall, crossing his ankles. "He'd have keys. He'd know how to bypass certain areas. He's been lying in wait."

Roman rolled his shoulders. "What's the plan? I have men on standby. Luca's away, but we're here." He gripped my shoulder. "We're getting her back. Tonight. He won't risk waiting."

"I know."

Evan walked in again. "Listen. When I had the drones at the racetrack last time, I landed a couple remote ones on the roof in case they were needed again. I've been busy and haven't recalled them. I just did a flyover. There's a car parked at the back—a dark sedan. And there are three heat sources, all in the one area." He showed it to Finn and me.

"That's where Lopez's office was located. He must have had a living space there too."

"That's where they are," I said. "It has to be."

"Then let's make a plan," Roman said. "Simple, quick, and quiet. In and out. We get Anna. We end Juan. Once and for all." He met my gaze, his furious. "We kill him so hard and bury him so deep, he'll never fucking crawl out. The bitch with him too."

I nodded. "Agreed."

CHAPTER SIXTEEN
ANNA

I heard them return, their footsteps echoing in the empty building. The closet door was flung open, and Juan stepped inside. He held a hammer in his hands. Fear built in my stomach.

What was he going to do with it?

He stood over me, sneering. "Heidi thought maybe you were too comfortable on the floor." He stepped over me, hammering a hook into the wall, then dragging me to my feet. I couldn't help the whimper that escaped my throat.

He liked that.

He loved it even more when he cut the cable ties from my hands, and I cried out as the pain rushed through the numb flesh. I felt my bracelet fall to the floor, and I had to let it go. He narrowed his eyes when he saw it, picking it up.

"Your precious Irishman give this to you?"

I stayed silent.

"He will pay for taking what is mine. Touching it."

He threw the bracelet back on the floor and smashed it with the hammer, not stopping until it was crushed. Ruined.

Useless.

Then he laughed and picked it up. "So poignant that this will represent you soon. And your Irishman will be dead."

"No," I gasped.

"Oh yes. We leave tomorrow for Colombia. And when he gets in his car next time—" he made a hand gesture "—*boom*. Both of them."

He leaned close, his hot breath hitting me. He stank of cigarettes and stale booze. "That's what he deserves."

"That's what you deserve."

He shook his head. He grabbed my hands, holding them at the front this time and wrapping another cable tie around them, tightening it until the plastic cut into my flesh. I cried out as he pushed my arms above my head, hooking the tie to the wall. "Heidi was right. You have a smart mouth we will have to beat out of you. And how we will enjoy it."

He stood back with a frown. "All of my marks are gone. Fading away. All the love marks I bestowed on you."

"You know nothing of love," I spat at him.

"I know you will worship me. Only me."

"Never."

He laughed, running his hand down my arms. I had to turn my head, hiding my revulsion. "When we arrive to your new home, your life will be mine. I am going to cover you in my marks. They will never be allowed to fade." He pinched me once, hard enough I whimpered. "And you will wear them like a badge of honor."

He walked away, leaving the door open. He flung himself onto the chair, pulling Heidi to his lap. She looked at me in triumph as she pulled his face to hers.

I shut my eyes and hung my head, concentrating on the pain and not them.

Tears slipped down my cheeks as I prayed for a miracle.

A miracle named Niall.

The next while, they acted as if I wasn't there, except on occasion when they said things to upset me. They argued a lot. Bickered—both wanting control. I wondered briefly if I could somehow use that to my advantage.

I hurt from standing, my shoulders screaming in pain. I was scared and cold. My head ached and I was exhausted. I was terrified of my future. Longing for Niall. His arms and the safety he provided.

Heidi lounged in a chair, making plans.

"I miss the pool." She turned to look at me. "Not that you'll be allowed to use it."

"As if I'd go into water you were in," I snapped. "That would be like blood to a great white shark. Although I understand they are intelligent animals."

Her eyes narrowed in annoyance, then she laughed. "Oh, bringing you to heel will be fun. I'm so glad I convinced Juan that we should have the fun of breaking you." She glanced at Juan. "Maybe instead of killing him right away, you should send him pictures of his precious Anna as she progresses into the perfect slave. That would hurt the doughy Irishman more than a bomb."

"Stop calling him that! Niall isn't *doughy*—he's a perfect specimen of a man."

Juan stormed in, grabbing my throat. "You will never speak his name again." He squeezed, cutting off my air. "He is nothing to you now. Do you understand?"

I gasped for air, unable to push his hands away.

Heidi laughed. "Don't kill her tonight. All this will be for nothing. Come to me, lover, and I will calm you."

Glaring, he walked out, slamming the door so hard it shook on the hinges.

I lowered my head, trying to catch my breath and ignore the sounds coming from the other room. A phone ringing interrupted them, and I was grateful. Juan spoke in another language then filled Heidi in.

"The plane will pick us up at seven tomorrow morning. We need to be ready."

Seven?

My heart sank.

Would Niall find me in time? I stared at the fragments of my bracelet on the floor and prayed I'd done enough.

If not, my life was over.

NIALL

We approached the racetrack on foot, parking far away so as not to arouse suspicion. There were only the four of us. Other men were already guarding the exits, keeping watch, making sure we got in safely. The moment Roman gave the signal, his men would move in.

But until then, we went in. Silent. Stealthy.

I saw the dark sedan, bending and confirming it was the same license plate as I had memorized from the video feed. Juan hadn't cared at that point about hiding himself or the car. He thought he had pulled it off. That we wouldn't be able to figure out where he was and that he had won.

Soon enough, he would know what he'd lost with his careless ego doing the thinking. Just like his uncle, he was lax.

In my ear, Aldo whispered confirmation the security was off for the door we approached, and he quickly picked the lock. Inside, we shut it behind us soundlessly and listened. From the outside, the racetrack appeared as it was supposed to be—deserted. Windows covered, no one around.

But in here, in the utter silence, we could hear it. Muted voices, footsteps.

I checked my gun and tugged on the straps of my vest. We were well armed, protected, and this time, not a silencer in sight. I wanted Juan to know the sounds of the gun that would kill him.

We knew the floor plan. Up the stairs and down the hall to the left. According to the blueprints our IT security team managed to produce, a set of living quarters was tucked behind the office Finn and I had been inside.

That was where they were.

We also had information on a small plane arriving early in the morning to transport them across the border. Another flight plan was found of them heading to Colombia.

None of them would be on time for that flight.

Two would be dead, and Anna would be where she belonged.

Safe in my arms.

Slowly, with utter precision, one by one, we crept up the cement stairs. Then we made our way through the door and down the hall. Ghosts, moving like shadows in the darkened corridor. A sliver of light spilled from a closed doorway. I could hear arguing coming from behind the door, one woman and one man.

We stopped and listened.

"If we drug her and put her in the suitcase again, there will be fewer questions. Less hassle."

"She has barely recovered from earlier. She is already half dead."

I froze, and Finn's hand landed on my shoulder.

Calm.

"She's pretending."

"The amount you would need to keep her knocked out is too risky. I've paid plenty for the loyalty of the pilot. He doesn't care if she's struggling and screaming. We can give her a dose before we land."

"It sounds as if you care too much for your little pet, Juan."

"I have risked everything to get her. To kill her before I enjoy it? No."

I'd heard enough.

Aldo bent, carefully sliding a tiny device under the door. Over his shoulder, I could see Juan standing with his back to the door. Heidi, who looked vastly different, stood across from him at the entrance to what looked like a closet. Her arms were crossed in anger. There was another door at the other end of the room.

I couldn't see Anna.

Aldo lifted his eyebrows. All three of them looked at me. It was risky to go in and not know where Anna was. Bursting through the door and firing meant she could be caught in the middle.

Finn pointed to the door where Heidi stood and pointed to himself. Then he indicated the other door, and I nodded. We'd each look for Anna behind those doorways.

I nodded and Aldo withdrew the device.

I held up my hand, all five fingers spread wide.

We positioned ourselves, guns drawn, nerves steady. We had the same goal.

In. Out. Done.

I counted down, lifting my gun as I closed my hand into a fist.

And we charged.

Aldo was first through the door, shooting Juan in the leg. He spun around like a ballerina, his arms raised, the look of shock on his face almost comical as he fell.

Roman followed, pinning him down, his gun on his forehead.

Finn charged toward the closet, as I tore through the room, looking for Anna.

"Niall," Finn spoke. "Here."

I passed Roman and Aldo, who were dragging Juan to his feet, him cursing and protesting.

"Handcuff him to the chair. Tape his mouth."

At the door, I froze. Heidi stood at the back of a closet, facing Finn and me, Anna in front of her, a knife to her throat. Anna's hands were tied in the front with cable ties, useless and injured. Her eyes were red-rimmed, and she was swaying on her feet. Fresh bruises and cuts marred her skin, and my rage became a living, breathing thing.

Finn's gun was aimed at Heidi, his arm steady. But the cowardly bitch knew exactly how to hold Anna for the most protection.

I met Anna's terrified eyes. They pleaded with me to help. To end this.

"Let her go, Heidi. This is not going to end well for you, and how it does is up to your next move."

She laughed. "Oh, you'll kill me, but I'll kill her first." She pressed the knife harder, a line of blood appearing on Anna's neck.

"Then we'll make it long and painful for you," Finn promised.

Heidi glared, and I saw Anna's eyes drop then flick back up, meeting mine. She dropped them again, and I saw Finn glance down. He gave a barely there tilt of his chin, and it happened.

Anna lifted her foot, stomping on Heidi's instep, making her shout, distracted. She grabbed at Anna, who bent low, falling to the side. Instantly, I lunged, grabbing Anna and pulling her out of the way as the sound of a gun echoed in the room.

I turned as Heidi slid to the floor, dead, the knife still clutched in her hand. Blood pooled around her head, her eyes staring ahead, lifeless.

Anna crumpled in my arms, and I held her as Finn dropped beside us, cutting off the cable ties. Her skin was bruised and broken in places, the unforgiving plastic embedded deeply.

I cupped her face. "I have you, *mo mhuirnín*. I have you."

She smiled, her lips trembling, her voice rough. "You found me."

I pressed a soft kiss to her lips. "Always."

She sighed a long exhale of air and went limp in my arms. I met Finn's gaze. "You take her. You keep her safe."

He indicated the other room. "I can do it, Niall. You stay with her."

I carefully transferred her to his arms. "No. I'm sending him to hell." I stood. "And this time, he's not coming back. But I don't want her waking and hearing what I do."

He nodded, lifting her slowly and following me.

Back in the garish room, I spoke to Aldo. "Go with Finn. Call your men."

"There is already a car downstairs. The men are waiting for their instructions," Roman stated.

"Make sure she is safe."

Aldo nodded. "With my life."

They left, and I heard the door click behind them.

"Take off the tape."

Juan's gaze was fixed behind me. I bent closer, meeting his angry gaze. "She's dead."

He stayed silent.

"Nothing to say? No weeping for your wife?"

"I have money. Contacts. Let me go, and I will never return. It was Heidi's idea to take her again," he begged.

It didn't really surprise me he was blaming a dead woman for his decisions, or that he would plead for his life. The fact that he didn't seem overly upset with her death was hardly a shock either. I doubted he truly cared for anyone but himself.

I looked at Roman. "Did you hear that? He'll never return."

Roman smirked.

I casually pointed my gun at his foot and shot it. He screamed, the sound music to my ears.

"That was for the mark on her cheek."

He panted, bending in pain.

I looked at him with a grimace. I had planned on having Roman take him somewhere. Let him rot in a dark prison the way he did to Anna. Torture him slowly.

But now, I just wanted him dead so I could get to Anna.

She needed me more than I needed him to suffer for weeks.

I pressed my gun to his left knee and planted another slug in him. He screamed again.

"That was for her left hand."

I did the same with his right knee, smirking when he could only whimper from the combined agony.

"That was for her right hand."

Then I hunched down in front of him. "Know this, Juan. The woman you decided to take and break? You failed. I'll make sure of that. I am going to love her the rest of her life. Watch over her. I will surround her in beauty. Drench her in happiness. While you're writhing in the fires of the underworld, know she'll be loved so deeply she won't even think about you anymore. Your name will fade from her mind. You'll be nothing but a bad dream. I'll make sure of that."

I stood. "Think about that as the devil finds you a special place in hell. Your name will be forgotten. You will be forgotten. And I'll have her. Always."

I pressed my gun to his head, meeting his eyes that were filled with hate. Rage. I smiled. "You lose, fecker."

I pulled the trigger, and he slumped in his chair, no longer a threat. Unable to stop, I added a slug to the place where, biologically, his heart would beat—if he'd ever had one.

The impact knocked him over, and he landed on his back, blood seeping into the carpet. I felt nothing but satisfaction that he was dead. Only regret it hadn't happened sooner.

Then I stepped back, ignoring the mess. If I could, I would have shot him all over again. Maybe that would be his punishment in hell. Reliving his death. It would be an appropriate way to spend eternity. At least in my opinion.

Roman met my eyes. "It's done."

He shook my shoulder. "Go. Anna needs you. We'll finish here."

"What are you planning?"

"Arson. The syndicate will have to rebuild." He glanced around. "Too much evil existed here."

I nodded. "Thank you."

He held out his hand. "Family," he said simply.

I shook it.

"Family."

CHAPTER SEVENTEEN
ANNA

I kept waking up, disjointed images and feelings swirling around me. Fear as I opened my eyes. Pain. Fragmented thoughts of being cold, terrified.

But every time I lifted my eyelids, *he* was there.

Niall.

Reassuring me in his low, rich voice.

Comforting me with his scent and gentle touch.

Watching me with his dark-brown eyes, caring and filled with love.

I was warm, my body cradled by softness and often his arms.

Sometimes I heard music. A sweet, familiar voice singing quietly. Gentle hands holding mine.

Still, I hid in the darkness, too scared to wake completely and find that I had been dreaming.

Until I heard it.

His whisper. His plea.

"*Come back to me,* mo mhuirnín. *I miss you. I need you.*"

I slowly opened my eyes, blinking at the light, grimacing at the brightness.

"I turned the light down," Niall's voice murmured. "Open your eyes for me."

I did, his face slowly coming into focus. He looked exhausted. Drawn. Anxious.

And he was the most beautiful thing I had ever seen.

"Niall?"

He cupped my cheek, bending over me. "*Mo mhuirnín.*" He pressed a kiss to my brow. "Thank God."

I peered around. I was in a hospital room, machines whirring and beeping. There was a sofa by the window and a large chair beside the bed where Niall had been sitting. Coffee cups were scattered on a table.

He smiled at my confusion. "You're in a private hospital. We brought you here after—" he swallowed "—after we got you out."

The whole ordeal rushed back, and my eyes widened, a flood of tears pouring down my cheeks. I gripped his wrists, panicking.

"No, Anna, hush," he soothed. "You're safe." He leaned close. "They are dead. They can't harm you again. No one will ever harm you again."

"But he...she... He was alive."

He pressed his lips to my ear. "I killed him. I made sure of it."

Something in his voice, his adamant words, made me relax.

"He said a bomb—your car," I babbled, feeling panicked.

"No. You already said something to Finn, and it's been checked. We're all safe, Anna."

I exhaled a shaky breath, another memory becoming clearer.

"Finn shot her," I whispered, recalling the closet.

"Yes."

"It's over?" I pleaded, gripping his shirt, trembling.

He sat on the bed, gently lifting me into his arms, crooning my name. "It's over."

And I wept.

The doctor came in, examined me, removed the oxygen, and capped off the IV. When I asked when I could leave, he patted my hand. "Soon."

I wanted soon to be now.

He spoke with Niall, then left. A few moments later, a nurse came in with a basin of warm water and some towels. She left after making sure I had ice water to drink and didn't need anything.

"How long was I out?" I asked, as Niall gently washed my face with a soft cloth.

He frowned. "Two days. The doctor was worried about your head, but they did a CT scan and there was no swelling in your brain. He told us you needed to rest, that your body needed the time to start healing." He met my eyes, his still anxious. "I hated seeing you like that."

"I know," I whispered, stilling his movements. "I'm okay, Niall."

"You will be," he assured me, bending down to press a tender kiss to my mouth. "I'll make sure of it."

"You said us."

"What?"

"You said 'the doctor told us.' Who is us?"

"Finn and Una were here until a few hours ago when you started to wake up. They thought we'd want privacy. Roman and Effie were here." He indicated flowers in the corner. "Aldo and Vi were here as well."

"Oh."

"Everyone was concerned."

"What about the hotel?"

He set aside the cloth and sat down. "It was obvious something had happened and it involved you. Finn told them there had been an attempted abduction, but you were safe. Everyone was horrified but so glad you're all right."

"Okay." I shifted, trying to pull myself up and grimacing.

He stood and helped me.

"My shoulders hurt the most."

He looked angry, but his voice was calm. "I know. I want you to stay on top of the pain meds. I hate seeing you in discomfort. When we get home, I'll have a massage therapist in for you daily."

I didn't respond, and he sat on the edge of the bed. "Are you coming home with me, Anna?"

"What?"

"I'm sure you're thinking how dangerous my world is now. If you've changed your mind—"

I stopped him by covering his mouth. "Stop it. Because of your world, I *am* here. Alive and with you. I was taken before I knew you. He came after me again because of his obsession. Both times, you rescued me. I'm grateful for *'your world.'*" I drew in a deep breath. "And I love you. I never want to leave you."

He was silent.

"I knew you'd come for me. Find me. I believed that the same way Una knew Finn would find her. Because of you, I had hope." I touched his hand. "And I was right. You found me."

I watched as emotions crossed his face. I was shocked to see tears in his eyes. He took my hand, kissing the palm and holding it to his cheek. "I thought I'd lost you. Even after we got you out, you were so lifeless in my arms—I was terrified." A tear rolled over my hand as he spoke. "I can't lose you, Anna. You have become so ingrained in my heart. The thought of anything happening to you tears me up inside, and I—"

I shook my head. "Then the safest place in the world for me is with you, isn't it?"

He inhaled, his emotions so clearly visible in his fierce expression. "Yes."

"Then the matter is settled. I'm staying with you, and you'll protect me and love me."

He smiled even as another tear splashed on my hand. "And you'll bake me cookies and love me."

"Always."

He rested his head on my chest, letting his emotions out. I stroked his hair, crooning softly, knowing I would be the only one he allowed to see his fear.

When he lifted his face, he met my eyes, his once again calm.

"Always."

Finn and Una came in, looking worried. I had moved to the chair, propped up with pillows, and Niall sat on the bed, feeding me tidbits of the food he had ordered in. I wasn't overly hungry, but I ate to please him.

Una saw I was awake and promptly burst into tears, racing to me and hugging me as she wept. I patted her back, grateful she was gentle. My shoulders and arms ached constantly. I let her cry, offering the box of tissues when she pulled back.

"I was so frightened," she whispered.

I squeezed her hand. "Me too."

Finn came over, bending and kissing my cheek. "Good to see you alert and sitting up."

"Thank you."

I glanced between him and Niall. "Maybe you two could go for coffee," I suggested. "Get Niall to eat something substantial, Finn." I indicated the morsels on the table. "He needs more than this."

Niall began to protest, and I smiled. "Una is here. You have a man outside. And I'd like to talk to my friend."

His face softened in understanding. He knew what a close bond I had with Una.

Finn nodded. "I brought food from the hotel for both of you. It's in the lounge."

Niall bent and kissed me. "Right down the hall."

"Okay."

Una held my hands. "She walked right past me...I didn't know."

"I know. Niall told me everything."

"I never liked her."

That made me chuckle. "I know."

"I wish I could slap her a few times," she confessed.

"Finn shot her."

She nodded. "He told me."

"Dead," I emphasized.

"I think that was the point."

"She was a bitch."

"Tell me."

I told her what I could recall. Some things were blurry. Some things too painful to relive, but I got them out. Una listened, letting me get all the words out in the open. She understood.

"Do you know what she called Niall?" I asked after we'd been quiet for a few moments.

"What?"

"Doughy."

Una frowned. "Doughy? What, compared to her stick of a wannabe man?"

"Exactly. I told her off."

"Bitch."

"She hit me."

"Finn killed her." She grinned. "He'd have killed her again if he'd heard that. He and Niall are a bit vain about their physique."

"As they should be."

We started to laugh, and it felt good.

She sighed. "Niall was beside himself. He loves you the way Finn loves me."

"I know."

"We're postponing the wedding."

"No, you can't. I'm fine. I can stand up for you—just maybe no pictures."

I had seen myself in the mirror. I was bruised, and I had a cut on my cheek where the bracelet had hit me. Another one by my mouth. A long one on my neck from the knife, which luckily was only surface, not a deep cut. But I wouldn't be camera-ready in a few days.

"We decided to go to Ireland first. See Roisin and let her have her party. Get married there unofficially, then come home and do it here. You'll have recovered more."

"I hate that you're putting it off for me."

"I realized I don't have to be married for Finn to be mine. He already is. So, whatever date the piece of paper says is just that. A date."

Then she smiled and winked. "And soon, we'll be planning yours."

I shrugged. "We haven't discussed that yet."

"You will."

NIALL

I glanced across at Anna who slept on the sofa. She was bundled up with blankets, warm and safe. Close. I needed her close at all times. Luckily, she felt the same way.

There was a knock at the door, and I hurried over, smiling when I saw it was Una.

"Come in. She's napping."

"Good. Finn needs you in the office. Roman is here with Aldo."

I looked over to Anna, hesitant.

"She'll be fine. I'll stay with her."

"I just ordered some lunch."

"Great. I'm starving."

I chuckled. "Okay, I'll get something with Finn."

She pushed her hair over her shoulder, her ring catching the light. She saw me looking at it with a smile.

"Something on your mind?" she asked playfully.

I tugged her into the hall. "I want to marry Anna."

"Good."

"I have no clue about a ring." I lifted her hand. "Would she like one like yours, maybe?"

She rolled her eyes. "Absolutely not. This rock would look wrong on Anna's hand. She is so small it would be an ice rink. It's even big for me, but Finn..." She trailed off with a shrug.

"What should I look for?"

She pulled out her phone. "I was hoping you'd ask. Just for fun, I got a bridal magazine the other day, and we went through it. Lots of ads for rings. Anna kept looking at one style in particular. I looked up the site for you." She handed me her phone.

I scrolled through the pictures. "They're, ah, small."

"No, the setting is delicate, but the diamond is still a nice size. The craftsmanship is exquisite." She tapped one picture. "Look at that pink diamond. And the rose gold setting. The intricate band. So romantic."

It was pretty. And Anna loved pink. "Um, so I order online?"

She huffed. "No, we'll go to a jeweler, and you can have it made."

"Probably a size six?" I guessed.

She sighed. "I wear a six and a half. She is a four."

"Ah."

"And she likes refined. Pretty. You get the best diamond you can. The very best."

I looked at her. "And you'll help."

She tapped something on her phone, waiting briefly. Then she squeezed my arm. "We'll go tomorrow. Finn will have lunch with her."

"So, he knows now?"

"Yes."

"Okay. Tomorrow it is."

Downstairs, I found Finn, Roman, and Aldo waiting for me. They had glasses of whiskey, and I helped myself to one.

"Please tell me this is a social visit," I said. "I can't take much more."

Roman chuckled. "In a way, yes. Everything is fine. Done. The official report was arson. No known suspects. The case is closed." He took a sip of his drink. "And the other is not an issue. It is as if they never existed, so we don't have to speak of it again."

"Good."

He cleared his throat. "Now, on to happy things. First off, I hear congratulations are in order."

I glared at Finn. "I haven't asked her yet."

"She'll say yes. It's just a formality," Finn replied with a wave of his hand.

Roman grinned, exchanging a glance with Aldo.

"I'm here to offer a wedding gift—well, to you both now."

Finn smiled. "Not necessary, but the thought is appreciated."

"Hear me out."

Finn nodded, waiting for Roman to speak.

"I know you're headed to Ireland and you're putting your official wedding off a bit."

"Yes."

"And you're going to cover while he is gone," he said to me.

"That's correct."

"I am offering you gentlemen Aldo."

Finn and I looked at each other.

"As a houseboy or something?" I asked, teasing.

He laughed and Aldo grinned. "No. I am going to run the Niagara hotel. Aldo will come here and run this one, and you *both* go to Ireland. Vi will come with him, and you'll provide a suite for them. You go see Roisin and leave the bad memories behind you. I think it would do you all a world of good. Give Anna a chance to heal. Have some alone time away from all this."

Finn cleared his throat. "That is very generous of you, but—"

Roman interrupted. "I want to do this." He indicated Aldo. "*We* want to do this."

"Why?"

He shrugged. "Because we're family now. Our women are friends. Effie understands what Anna and Una have been through. Her loving heart is breaking for Anna, and she wanted to do something. She reminded me of the gift of time I gave Luca when he got married. And Aldo. That gift was returned by them when Effie and I went away for a while. We needed it. I would say you need it."

Finn looked stunned. "I don't know what to say, Roman."

"Say yes. We'll agree on dates and move forward. I assume all is peaceful again in your territories?"

"Yes."

"Great. Your men can handle things, and we'll only step in if needed. Aldo will be here in case your management requires him, and you can take Una and Anna to Ireland. Whisk them to a castle or some other place. Indulge them. Indulge yourself. We'll handle things here."

"We'll return the favor if ever needed."

"It's a gift, not a favor, but we'll keep it in mind." He stood, extending his hand. "Agreed?"

We took turns shaking hands. "Agreed."

Una and Anna were baking cookies when we returned to the suite. I inhaled the scent of sugar and chocolate as we walked in. I bent and kissed Anna. "You look better," I murmured.

Every day, she got a little stronger. Less pale and tense-looking. I was hoping the news we were about to share would make her smile.

"This is a treat," I added, taking a cookie. "Delicious too." I bit into the warm dough.

Finn hummed around his mouthful, as pleased as I was to see them looking happy and relaxed.

"I have some good news," he announced.

"Do tell," Una said, sliding the cookies into a canister.

He explained Roman's offer, and I watched Anna carefully to see her reaction.

"I've never been to Ireland," she said, clasping her hands. "Really?" She turned to me. "We could see your mum? I could meet her?"

They had spoken on the phone. FaceTimed as well.

Mum already loved her, and I knew she'd be thrilled to meet her and welcome her to the family officially.

I nodded. "The best part is she could come back with us to be here for Finn's wedding."

Una clapped her hands in glee. "That is perfect!"

"We'll spend time with Roisin and do a little traveling alone," Finn said. "Roman is giving us three weeks."

"Can we see London? I've always wanted to see London," Una asked, her eyes bright with excitement.

He wrapped his arm around her, pulling her close and kissing her. "Yes."

I looked at Anna, already knowing she wouldn't want to be in a big city. "What about you?" I asked quietly. I had an idea, and I made a suggestion. "Would a quiet place in the country suit you?"

"Yes," she sighed. "I'd prefer that."

"I'll make the arrangements."

"When do we leave?"

"A week."

Una grabbed Finn's hand. "We have so much to do! We need to start planning."

He grabbed another cookie on the way out. I turned to

Anna, opening my arms, smiling as she nestled into my chest, her head pressed into her favorite spot.

"We'll go and find some quiet spot to relax in," I promised, already knowing the place. "You can recover, and I'll be right beside you."

She looked up, her eyes bright. "Loving me."

I bent and kissed her.

"Always."

THE FINAL CHAPTER
NIALL

I woke, my hand searching for Anna. Her side of the bed was empty, and I sat up, listening. She wasn't in the bathroom. I shrugged on my robe and headed to the living room. She was standing in front of the window, looking outside, her forehead pressed against the glass.

I walked up behind her, pulling her into my arms. "You were gone."

"I couldn't sleep."

"Nervous about flying?" She had never been on a plane. Never left the province.

"A little."

"It's private. No strangers. Only us."

"I know." She smiled softly. "And the newlyweds."

Finn hadn't been able to wait. He'd married Una in a private ceremony on his terrace, with Anna and me as witnesses. He insisted he'd waited for too long already, and Una didn't object. They still planned a party in Ireland and another when we came home. But that moment, that day, was for them. They married at dawn, then disappeared for the next thirty-six hours. Finn appeared at his desk after lunch, looking like Finn, except with a contented, happy expression. And a wide gold band on his left hand.

We had put the trip off for two more weeks, wanting Anna healed and to make sure everything was covered here. I had been counting the days.

I searched my brain. "What is making you so nervous, then?"

She sighed, and I held her tighter. "Tell me. Let me fix it."

She met my eyes in the glass. "You always want to fix it."

"Yes."

"What if, once she meets me, your mum doesn't like me?"

I barked out a laugh. "Impossible. She was so happy about Finn and Una. When I told her about you, she was beside herself. You've talked to her. Several times.

FaceTimed her. She is crazy about you already." I bent and kissed her neck. "You love her son. You make him so happy, she couldn't help but love you."

"It's so fast. What if she..." Anna shrugged. "Once she meets me, she might change her mind."

"Impossible," I repeated. "She will love you even more. She is so excited. Finn and Una married, me bringing home the woman I love—" I stopped speaking. "No, wait."

"What?" she murmured.

"Let's change up the dialogue."

She frowned, her reflection confused. "What?" she said again.

I slipped the box from my pocket where I had it hidden and held it in front of her. "I think with Finn married, I should bring home my fiancée."

She stared down at the box, not touching it. I turned her in my arms and held the box out again. "Please. Marry me."

She looked up, tears glistening. "Niall," she murmured. "Are you sure?"

I tipped up her chin and kissed her, a gentle press of my mouth to hers. "I am more certain of marrying you than I have ever been of any decision in my life. I was meant to be the one who rescued you. You were meant to be mine. I want to take you to Ireland and introduce you to Mum as my intended." I kissed her again. "I'd like to marry you there, but they have a strict three-month waiting period."

She gazed up at me, love shining in her eyes. She clutched the intricately carved box in her hands, cradling it as if it were the most precious thing in the world.

"Really?"

I smiled. "You have to say yes first. And look at your ring."

"Yes."

"Open your ring, *mo mhuirnín,*" I instructed gently.

She paused, biting her lip, then opened the lid and gasped. I grinned at her reaction. I took the box from her hand, sliding the ring onto her finger. "Perfect."

I had chosen a flawless two-carat diamond set in white gold with rose gold accents. The band was intricate and dotted with tiny diamonds set among leaves and tiny flowers. The wedding band I would add soon went around the ring, encasing it on both sides with more elaborate work and completing a Celtic knot on either side of the center diamond. It was unique, beautiful, and one of a kind—just like the woman I was going to marry.

"It's the most beautiful ring I have ever seen," she whispered.

"Una helped me. She said you wouldn't like one like hers. I thought this one would suit you."

"It's so..." She looked up. "Niall, I love it. It's perfect. I love you."

"So, that would still be a yes?" I teased.

"Oh! Yes! Yes!" She flung her arms around me, and I held her close, thrilled with her reaction, her answer, and the fact that my mum would be beyond ecstatic.

I pressed a kiss to Anna's head. "It's gonna be an amazing trip," I promised. "Mum is going to love you even more than she already does. I'll show you Ireland. I get you all to myself for ten days." I grinned. "That is the best part."

She snuggled close. "Yes, it is."

"Ready to come back to bed? I have this urgent need to make love to my fiancée. Help her relax."

"Oh," she murmured, pressing closer and feeling my need. "*Oh*. Yes."

I lifted her into my arms and carried her back to bed.

TWO WEEKS LATER

I stood by the bar, the noise and merriment filling the pub endless. Music was being played, the fiddle and drums beating out a lively tune. Tables groaned with food. Mum's friends, neighbors, and locals blended. Far too much whiskey and liquor were being consumed. The laughter was loud and boisterous.

And I was smiling so widely, my face hurt. I watched my shy, timid Anna dance with one stranger, then another. She was passed around like a box of chocolates on Christmas Day. One hand to the next—and she was fine. More than fine. She was happy, relaxed. Laughing, her head thrown back, her long hair brushing the top of her sweetly curved ass. She wore a dress Mum had bought her—a throwback to medieval days with a long white blouse-thing underneath and a vivid blue front-laced corset-type style over the top. The blouse had long, lacy sleeves, and the front dipped low with another froth of lace. The dress had slits up the front, flashing her legs as she danced, and Anna was beyond sexy in it. Una was beside her, dressed the same, but hers was green. With her red hair, she was the perfect Irish lass, yet nothing could hold a candle to my Anna. Mum was on the other side of the room, clapping and laughing, her eyes full of love for her two new daughters. Even though Anna and I weren't married yet legally, Mum didn't care. She adored them both, but she loved Anna with a fierceness only a mother could have, and I was happy to see how well they got along.

Finn came up beside me, leaning on the bar. "Grand," he murmured. "What a fecking grand day."

I laughed. "Anna mentioned how strong your brogue is again—she's right."

"You should hear yourself." He chuckled and threw back his whiskey. "Roisin throws quite the party."

"That she does."

"Anna looks incredible. So happy."

"So relaxed," I added. "No nightmares, no worries, nothing here." I took a sip of my drink. "I hope it continues."

"Same for Una. She isn't afraid of anything here."

I chuckled. "Maybe because the two of them have charmed the whole population of the town. No one would get near them without being torn to shreds by the locals."

Finn laughed in agreement. "Especially the males. Look at Tim Driscoll. Eighty years of age and he's dancing with our women like someone half his age. If someone came at them, he'd fight like a champ."

"Maybe we should stay here," I murmured.

Finn blinked. "Really?"

I shrugged. "If Anna were happier here, I'd move in a heartbeat. Luckily, she doesn't want to." I eyed him. "You'd do the same for Una."

"I would." He winked. "Lucky for me too, she doesn't want to stay either. But the break has been good for them." He paused. "Us too."

I added more whiskey to our glasses. "Did Mum tell you she got the green light to come back with us? She'll be there for my wedding. And your party."

"She did. Una and I are thrilled. I hope we can get her to stay for a while."

"She's bringing Connie and Maggie with her," I informed him, referring to her two best friends.

"Jesus. They almost killed us last time."

I threw back my head in amusement. "This time, Una and Anna can help. And we can beg Roman to let them stay at his hotel for a few days. Gamble and see the sights. Give us a much-needed break."

Finn shook his head. "Jesus, Mary, and Joseph. I'll owe the man so much, I'll never be able to pay him back."

Then his face softened as he looked back at the dance floor. "But worth it." I followed his gaze. Mum was on the dance floor now with the girls, teaching them some Irish steps. All three were laughing with their arms around one another as they tried to follow her footwork.

"That is as grand a sight as I ever saw," I muttered. "Who knew all it took to make Mum happy was to be happy ourselves?"

Finn threw his arm over my shoulder. "Who knew, indeed. Let's go show these women how it's done."

I side-eyed him. "How drunk are you? You haven't tried an Irish jig since we were kids."

"No time like the present."

The way Anna was beckoning to me with her beautiful eyes and her hand outstretched, I decided he was right. I downed the last of my whiskey.

"Let's go."

I woke the next morning facedown on my bed. I was stretched across the mattress, clad only in my boxers. There was a god-awful racket coming from somewhere in the room, and when I pulled myself up,

I discovered Finn passed out on the floor, a blanket over him, snoring like he was a seventy-year-old man with a smoking addiction.

I sat up carefully, not wanting to make the jackhammers in my head any louder.

Where the feck was Anna, and why was Finn on the floor?

I stood on my shaky legs and kicked his foot. He made a strange sound and rolled over, the snoring immediately starting again.

I pulled on some sweats and went to the bathroom, emptying my bursting bladder, brushing my teeth, splashing cold water on my face to try to wake up. I took some pain meds and looked at myself in the mirror.

I hadn't looked this hungover in decades.

I made my way downstairs, wondering if I had been in a car accident. My legs ached as hard as my head. I found Anna, Una, and Sully with Mum in the bright kitchen, a pot of tea on the table, the scent of fresh bread in the air.

"Morning," I rasped out.

All four looked at me, then started to laugh. Anna came over, placing her hand on my chest. "Niall, it's one o'clock. In the afternoon," she added in case I didn't understand.

"Holy feck," I muttered.

"Is Finn alive?" Una asked with a grin.

"Since he's doing an imitation of a piece of heavy machinery, I assume so," I said, sitting down. "What the feck happened last night?"

Mum slid a cup of tea in front of me. I wanted coffee, but considering everything, I decided not to ask. At least the tea was hot and strong. She shook her head. "You and Finn got into a drinking game. You drank shots of whiskey and challenged each other to, ah, an Irish dance-off." She bit her lip. "It was one for the record books, my boy."

"I haven't Irish danced since I was a kid and you made me take lessons," I protested, horrified.

"Apparently you remembered some of them. As did Finn."

"The rest," Sully finished with a smirk, "you made up with great gusto. I had no idea you could do the splits, Niall."

I leaned my head on the table. "Feck. Neither did I." No wonder my legs ached. Then I lifted my head. "Who won?"

"It was a draw. When the table you insisted on using collapsed under the weight of the two of you stomping on it like you were cast members of

Riverdance, we called it," Anna said, her eyes twinkling.

"I'm sure we were excellent," I protested.

Mum snorted. "More arm-flinging and kicking like donkeys than dancing, really."

I sputtered into my tea, choosing to ignore her even as they all laughed.

"And why is Finn on the floor?"

"Anna managed to get you to bed, and Finn came in to tell you something. He just sort of dumped himself there, and we decided to leave him when he started snoring," Una informed me. "What a racket. I had no idea."

"Too late," Finn's rough voice spoke from the door. "You married me. You're stuck with me."

He looked as awful as I felt. He sat next to Una, placing his head on her shoulder. "Oh, you reek," she laughed. "Whiskey, cigars, and regret."

"Help me," he pleaded.

Mum stood. "Right. A good breakfast will sort you out. We have a lot to do today. You leave tomorrow, and I'll not have you off with a hangover."

I met Finn's bloodshot eyes. He narrowed his and mouthed the words "I won."

I shook my head. "Nope."

"Rematch," he muttered, then paused and rubbed his legs. "Never mind."

We all started to laugh. I glanced at Sully, who nodded, letting me know all was set. Finn and Una were off to London for a week. I was taking Anna to Sully's cottage. A week of peace, quiet, and privacy. I hadn't told her, wanting it to be a surprise.

I only hoped I was recovered enough by tomorrow to enjoy it.

Thanks to Mum's hearty breakfast and an early night —this time sleeping with Anna—I felt fine the next day. We made our way to Dublin, kissing Mum goodbye with plans for her to meet us in seven days at the airport. Once we arrived, we dropped Finn and Una off at his favorite hotel for a couple of days, then headed to the airport. The jet flew Anna and me to Edinburgh. The pilot would return to Dublin and take Finn and Una to London in a couple of days. We caught a train to the small village, Anna still in the dark about where we were going. We strolled through the quaint town, taking in the quiet streets and friendly people. Using the directions Sully had given me, I guided Anna to the shore's edge, and we stared out at the expanse of water before us. Then I turned her, pointing to the small stone cottage. "There, *mo mhuirnín.* That's our place for the next while."

She clasped her hands in delight and raced up the shore to the path. Laughing, I followed, holding on to the small case we'd brought. I opened the door for her with a flourish. "Ta-da!"

Inside, we looked around. The living area walls were whitewashed, the old floorboards gleaming in the afternoon sun that streamed in from the expansive windows. Hand-braided rugs felt cozy under our feet. The fireplace was stone like the outside, the hearth a huge piece of timber. Two large wingback chairs were by the fireplace, and a small sofa sat in front of it. Sully had told me he added the wing chairs so he had somewhere to sit. The sofa was too small for him. I assumed he would change that eventually.

The cottage had a center hall—to one side, a kitchen, and the other, a bathroom and the only bedroom. That room held a queen-sized bed, a small wardrobe, and a nightstand. The quilt on the bed was handmade and faded, but the room was welcoming, done in cream and green.

"Sully has applied for planning permission to add to the back of the cottage and make this bigger," I told

Anna. "He needs a king-sized bed. And he wants a closet."

Off the kitchen was a small conservatory where a table and a couple of chairs were set up. "He'll add to this as well, he tells me."

"It's so perfect," Anna murmured. "Cozy and warm. I can't wait to see the sunrises from that porch."

"I can't wait to make love to you in front of that fireplace," I said, wrapping her in my arms. "On that bed. Maybe the counter. By the water."

"Planning ahead, are we?"

I laughed. "No one around to hear us. No Mum downstairs, no Finn next door trying to figure out the same thing—how to shag our women without making a sound."

"You were pretty inventive."

"Not often enough," I growled, picking her up. "We have lots of time to make up for. And we're starting now."

She cupped my face. "Okay, Mr. Black. Do your worst."

I woke up, already knowing the bed would be empty. Every day, Anna got up and watched the sunrise, a cup of tea in her hand, a smile on her face. She loved it here. The peace and quiet. The people. The privacy. She went for walks by herself often—strolling into the village to pick up something sweet for dessert or to say hello to the group of old women she'd made friends with. I'd followed her the first time, stealthy and unseen.

Until she called me out on it on the way back.

"Don't give up your day job, Niall," she called out. *"Leave the stalking to the professionals."*

That was the day I made love to her on the porch after chasing her.

I sat up, feeling the sadness of knowing it was our last full day, but the excitement of knowing we were headed back home. We could get married. Start our life.

I pulled on my sweats and headed outside. Today, she stood on the shore, staring at the water. The last of the dawn was dissipating in the sky, the colors fading into light. I stepped behind her, wrapping my arms around her. "Hello, *mo mhuirnín*."

She patted my arm. "Hello, handsome."

I pressed a kiss to her head. "What are you thinking?" I asked after a few moments.

"Wishful thoughts."

"Share them with me."

"That we could stay forever."

Her voice was sad, making me frown. She wanted to stay here? Scotland?

I turned her in my arms. "Here, Anna? Is this where you feel safe?" I swallowed. "I can arrange it with Finn. I—"

She cut me off. "No, no. I meant here—in this moment. When we're happy. In love."

"That isn't going to change. I'm going to love you the rest of my life."

"I know. But not this way. All-consuming, passionate. Where you can't wait to see the other person. When romance takes precedence over everything else."

"Exactly that way," I insisted.

She smiled. "I hope so."

I tilted my head and pulled a box from my pocket. I had been debating showing this to her, but right now, romance was going to take the precedence she wanted.

"What is that?" she asked.

I opened the lid. "Your wedding band. Mine to match."

Her eyes widened.

"Give me your ring."

Hesitating, she slid it off her finger, offering it to me. I handed her my much larger ring. "Hold that."

She watched as I slipped her ring into the center of the two connected bands, forming a flowing pattern and making the Celtic knot complete.

I lifted her hand and kissed it, then slid the rings back onto her finger. I met her wide gaze.

"Years ago, people exchanged vows privately. So today, Anna, I take you as my wife. I will love you, protect you, and forever make sure our romance is alive and well. You will never be alone. I will always be there to hold your hand, kiss you, and consume you with passion any time you want. Or when I want." I winked at her. "We'll figure it out." I took a deep breath. "For as long as I live."

Her fingers trembled as she slipped the white gold band on my finger. "I take you, Niall, today, to be my husband. I will love you all the days of my life. No matter where we go, I'll be home because you'll be with me." Tears formed in her eyes and flowed down her cheeks. "Always."

I bent and kissed her. "Always."

We celebrated on the flight once Una noticed our bands. Finn had the attendant bring champagne, and we toasted over and over. When Mum and her cronies fell asleep, Finn nudged my leg with his foot. "I spoke to Roman yesterday. He had an offer."

"Another one?"

He laughed. "I think this came from the women. They would like to host the party and were wondering how you felt about getting married overlooking the Falls, then combining the party into a reception for us both."

I glanced at Anna. She wanted a small wedding, much the same as Una had.

"Can we keep it minimal?"

He nodded. "Us, Roisin and company, plus the trio and wives." He chuckled. "And his nonna. The guest list for the party is up to us. And if you're not interested, not an issue."

I turned to Anna. "Your call, *mo mhuirnín.*"

Una spoke. "Effie said she would handle everything. All we have to do is turn up in pretty dresses. You two say your vows—legally. Sign the papers, and then we party."

Anna looked thoughtful, her chin resting on her hand. The light caught on the new bracelet I had given her, equipped with another tracker. I'd felt better once I'd placed it on her wrist, and she did as well. "On two conditions."

"Which are?" I asked. I wanted to make sure she was happy.

"That you sing for us," Anna murmured, looking at Una.

Una took her hand. "Yes."

"And the second?" I prompted.

"No Irish dance contests," she said with a chuckle.

Finn and I laughed. "That will never happen again. My legs haven't recovered yet."

I pulled her close. "Are you sure, Anna?"

"As long as I get to marry you again, I'm sure. Niagara Falls is romantic."

I kissed her. "Then let's get married. Again."

She snuggled close.

"Always."

Anna was a beautiful bride. Not that I'd had any doubts, but she was beyond perfect. With her long hair flowing down her back and dressed in a pretty pink dress that exploded from her waist in a froth of lace, she was a vision.

Roman walked her down the short aisle, placing her hand into mine. He was very fond of her, acting like the brother she missed—protective and caring. I was grateful for his presence in her life, knowing he would always watch over her if I wasn't around. She could depend on him—we both could.

Our vows were short and simple, each of us planning on repeating the ones we'd made in private. I gazed down at my bride, and a wave of emotion hit me as I spoke. "Anna, you have completed my life. Made it full and rich. The parts of me I thought were broken you mended and made whole. I will love you fiercely until the day I depart from this earth." I bent low, wiping a tear from her eye. "Every chance I get, I will love you."

That made our small group laugh and Anna's smile widen. Her dimple popped, and I knew she liked my promises. All of them.

Her words were much the same as they had been that

day in Scotland, the love she carried for me soaked into her words.

I kissed her after, ignoring the clearing of the clergyman's throat. I had to. She was too beautiful to resist.

I stepped back and he sighed. "I now pronounce you husband and wife. You may kiss your bride—again."

And I did so with great gusto.

We had a private dinner, then headed to the room Roman had chosen for our reception. It was filled with other syndicate members, their families, some friends, and Roman's crew and family. There was dancing and laughter. Some speeches. A beautiful cake.

And I got to dance with my wife. With her head nestled onto my chest, we swayed, our bodies pressed together. She wasn't as relaxed as she had been in Ireland, but she was gracious and kind to everyone who congratulated us, accepting their well-wishes warmly. Still, when she asked how long we had to stay, I was only too pleased to tell her we could leave anytime.

No one would blame me for wanting my wife to myself.

I bent and kissed her. "A few more dances, *mo mhuirnín*. I know Finn wants to dance with you, and I need to take Mum for another turn on the dance floor." I tickled her chin. "And I don't think Roman would forgive me if I whisked you away without a dance."

"Okay." She beamed up at me.

"Then we'll go. Tomorrow, we start a new chapter, yes?"

"Yes."

"Our story is just beginning, Anna. And a happily ever after is guaranteed. I'll make sure of it."

Her dimple appeared again. "I know," she whispered. "I love you."

I bent and pressed my mouth to hers. "Always."

FINN

Five years later

Roman looked over the documents, nodding as he closed the file. "Basically, the same transfer of power as we did with you," he said.

"It is."

"They were the first to offer men and support with the Una situation," he mused.

"And his territories butt up against mine. He'll simply absorb them under his protection." I paused. "I like him as well. Marco Serrano has been nothing but up-front in his dealings."

He rubbed his chin thoughtfully. "That was much the same as I felt about you. But you don't have to consult me on this, Finn. I'm not part of the syndicate anymore."

I laughed, picking up my coffee cup and taking a sip. "I'm aware. But we're friends. Colleagues. I trust your judgment."

He smiled. "Our wives would say more than friends." He took a drink of his coffee. "I suppose I would as well."

In the years since Una had been taken, a strong relationship had developed between our families. Our wives were friends. We had become friends. Holidays and celebrations were shared.

It was unusual, but not unheard of within the syndicate.

He looked around. "I noticed no mention was made of O'Reilly's."

I shook my head. "I'm keeping it. I have the right management in place to run it day-to-day. I've hired a great overseer for the casino. Very personable. She came highly recommended and has impressed me. I'll come into the city every week to handle anything necessary, but otherwise, I'll be a figurehead." I drained my cup. "And I will keep my suite in case we want to come into town and stay. And Una can sing when she wants to."

He shook his head. "You really plan on staying home with Nolan?"

Simply the mention of my son's name made me smile. Nolan James O'Reilly had screamed his way into the world and immediately burrowed himself into my heart. The moment I held him, I knew I wanted him to have more than I had as a child. I wanted to give him choices. Options I was never given. I didn't want him brought up in a world of danger.

Long before we'd learned she was pregnant, Una and I had been in Niagara-on-the-Lake for a break. Out for a walk, we'd found a huge old Victorian house for sale.

Una stood staring at it, and I knew she'd found her dream property. I bought it for her, and we spent millions renovating it and turning it into a small boutique hotel. Ten rooms, each one unique. A dining room that was so sought-after, it had a waitlist of over a year. Guests were given a reservation with their room, and locals lined up hoping a client wouldn't use their given time slot, but it rarely happened. Five tables were available for non-hotel guests, and there was never an empty spot. Una ran the hotel like a seasoned pro, and I was so proud of her I couldn't contain it.

We'd also bought a piece of land not far from Roman's estate and built a house. I didn't want her commuting every day, and I started adjusting my time spent in Toronto, unknowingly starting the process of distancing myself.

Once we discovered she was pregnant, I knew my time with the syndicate was ending. I began the quiet course of finding the right person to take over my spot within the organization. I'd planned on working full time, but once my son was born, I decided he was more important. Una loved what she did. She thrived living her lifelong dream, and I didn't want to take that from her.

So, for the next while, I would be a hotel owner and full-time caregiver to my son.

The door opened, and Niall strolled in, a baby carrier strapped to his chest, his baby daughter snuggled safely in the material. She was the spitting image of Anna, from her golden curls to her tiny form. Niall was as enraptured with her as he was with her mother.

I chuckled at the sight, although it wasn't a rare one. He was as hands-on with his child as I was with mine. An added bonus was that I was her godfather, and I took the honor seriously. She had two very protective men watching over her.

"Everything okay?" I asked.

He grinned, stroking the soft curls on Keira's head. "Anna's overseeing the packing."

Roman stood, peering down at Keira. She was six months older than Nolan. Anna and Una were still incredibly close, and I was certain would remain so the rest of their lives. It somehow didn't surprise anyone when they were both pregnant so close together.

"Keep the babies away from Effie," he groaned. "She's been talking about another one, thanks to you lot. I'm too old for another child, and I have no desire to have my vasectomy reversed. My two keep me plenty busy. Plus, Aldo's kids are always at my place, so it's crazy with five of them running around, taking over the house all the time."

We laughed, knowing he didn't mean any of it. If Effie wanted another child, he'd make it happen. And he loved the "houseful," as he called them.

Niall sat down, cradling his daughter close, his tenderness for her apparent.

"Anna is so excited about moving," he said, pointing to the coffeepot. I poured him a cup, and he took a long sip. "Being close to Una again." He flashed a grin at Roman. "And Effie and Vi."

He chuckled. "We'll all be close now." He sat back, resting his ankle on his knee. "Who knew all this would happen when we handed the territory over to you, Finn." He waved his hand. "Some hellish moments, but what we've gained..." His smile was warm. "Priceless."

Niall lifted a tiny hand to his mouth, kissing the knuckles of his daughter as he nodded, looking thoughtful. I knew he was thinking about Anna. She was never far from his thoughts. He was a devoted husband and father.

And I was anxious to return home, knowing Una and Nolan would be waiting for me. I still hated being away from Una, and now, with Nolan, I loathed leaving them at all. They were my entire world and always would be.

Our lives had changed, become richer because of the women we loved and the friends we had made.

And I was looking forward to the future. One free of the darker side of the world I'd lived in for so long. Filled with love. Laughter. More children.

I met Niall's eyes, and we shared a silent conversation.

He was a constant by my side. Always loyal, always ready to follow my lead. More than a cousin—he was my brother.

It was time for a new path. For both of us. I owed him that, at the very least. Much more, actually, but we'd start there.

I tapped the file on my desk.

"I'll finish this. As soon as possible."

Niall stood and shook my hand. "To the future."

I nodded. "The future."

Roman joined us. "It's never looked brighter."

And as if to make sure we knew she had an opinion, Keira opened her eyes and made a little noise, lifting her fist and waving it, making us all grin. Niall tapped her knuckles. "We hear you, princess."

Right there was our future.

Bright, indeed.

Aren't you glad I made you wait for the epilogue? I enjoyed writing these men in their happily ever afters.

Thank you for reading NIALL. If you are so inclined, reviews are always welcome by me at your retailer.

If you'd like to read more about Aldo and Roman, their stories are in the Men of the Falls duet available in ebook, paperback and audiobook.

Enjoy meeting other readers? Lots of fun, with upcoming book talk and giveaways! Check out Melanie Moreland's Minions on Facebook.

Join my newsletter for up-to-date news, sales, book announcements and excerpts (no spam). Click here to sign up Melanie Moreland's newsletter or use the QR code below:

Scan To Sign Up Now

Visit my website www.melaniemoreland.com
Enjoy reading! Melanie

ACKNOWLEDGMENTS

Many thanks to many people.

My team and admins work together to ensure my group, page and SM runs while I am busy creating. Their tasks are endless, their jobs thankless. But without them I would be lost.

Emily, Atlee, Karen, and George thank you.

My Hype team is filled with wonderful people who shout about my books, squeal over arcs and keep me uplifted when I'm uncertain. I am so grateful for you ladies—much love to you.

Beth, Deb, Sisters D & D—thank you for your eyes, your support, and your suggestions. They make my books better.

Lisa—you rock. That is all I have to say. That and the diet coke is always on ice for you.

Karen—there are no words—even for me. My right hand, my left, my sister from another mister. You make my book world easier and my real world brighter. Love you.

The bloggers, the readers, the posters and the reviewers. Thank you for being part of this journey.

And to my Matthew—Love. Always Love. Thank you for the thousand and one things you do to make sure I get to spend time with my characters, even if it means less time with you. I am lucky to call you mine.

ALSO AVAILABLE FROM MORELAND BOOKS

Titles published under Melanie Moreland

The Contract Series

Marriage of Convenience- Same Couple

The Contract (Contract #1)

The Baby Clause (Contract Novella)

The Amendment (Contract #3)

The Addendum (Contract #4)

Vested Interest Series

Billionaire - Different Couples

BAM - The Beginning (Prequel)

Bentley (Vested Interest #1)

Aiden (Vested Interest #2)

Maddox (Vested Interest #3)

Reid (Vested Interest #4)

Van (Vested Interest #5)

Halton (Vested Interest #6)

Sandy (Vested Interest #7)

Vested Interest/ABC Crossover

A Merry Vested Wedding

ABC Corp Series

Second Generation - Different Couples

My Saving Grace (Vested Interest: ABC Corp #1)

Finding Ronan's Heart (Vested Interest: ABC Corp #2)

Loved By Liam (Vested Interest: ABC Corp #3)

Age of Ava (Vested Interest: ABC Corp #4)

Sunshine & Sammy (Vested Interest: ABC Corp #5)

Unscripted With Mila (Vested Interest: ABC Corp #6)

Men of Hidden Justice

Vigilante Justice - Different Couples

The Boss

Second-In-Command

The Commander

The Watcher

The Specialist

Men of the Falls

Canadian mafia duet - Different Couples

Aldo

Roman

The Irishmen

Canadian syndicate duet - Different Couples

Finn

Niall

My Favorite

Romantic Comedy standalone

My Favorite Kidnapper

My Favorite Boss

My Favorite Hero

Reynolds Restorations -

Blue Collar heroes in Small Town - Different Couples

Revved to the Maxx

Breaking The Speed Limit

Shifting Gears

Under The Radar

Full Throttle

Standalones

Tropes from high angst to romcom

Into the Storm

Beneath the Scars

Over the Fence

The Image of You

Changing Roles

The Summer of Us

Happily Ever After Collection

Heart Strings

A Simple Life

Titles published under M. Moreland

Insta-Spark Collection

Low Angst and all standalone

It Started with a Kiss

Christmas Sugar

An Instant Connection

An Unexpected Gift

Harvest of Love

An Unexpected Chance

Following Maggie

The Wish List

Wrapped In Love

ABOUT THE AUTHOR

NYT/WSJ/USAT international bestselling author Melanie Moreland, lives a happy and content life in a quiet area of Ontario with her beloved husband of thirty-plus years and their rescue cat, Amber. Nothing means more to her than her friends and family, and she cherishes every moment spent with them.

While seriously addicted to coffee, and highly challenged with all things computer-related and technical, she relishes baking, cooking, and trying new recipes for people to sample. She loves to throw dinner parties, and enjoys traveling, here and abroad, but finds coming home is always the best part of any trip.

Melanie loves stories, especially paired with a good wine, and enjoys skydiving (free falling over a fleck of dust) extreme snowboarding (falling down stairs) and piloting her own helicopter (tripping over her own feet.) She's learned happily ever afters, even bumpy ones, are all in how you tell the story.

Melanie is represented by Flavia Viotti at Bookcase Literary Agency. For any questions regarding subsidiary or translation rights please contact her at flavia@bookcaseagency.com

- facebook.com/authormoreland
- instagram.com/morelandmelanie
- bookbub.com/authors/melanie-moreland
- amazon.com/Melanie-Moreland/author/B00GV6LB00
- goodreads.com/Melanie_Moreland
- tiktok.com/@melaniemoreland
- threads.net/@morelandmelanie